by Michelle Stimpson

Acknowledgements

Thanks and honor be to the Lord for all His goodness. Writing for His glory is my pleasure and joy. I'm honored to be in His service through this and many other venues.

Thanks to my family, friends, and the writers who continue to inspire me. A special "thanks" to Allison at Care Now Clinic, who freely shared information that helped make me understand how emergency clinics work.

Finally, to those dedicated readers who continue to support my books. I dedicate this book to you!

Chapter 1

The party was a huge success. Knox Stoneworth's parents, Reth and Carolyn, had celebrated thirty-five years of marriage surrounded by everyone they loved—brothers, sisters, cousins, aunts, uncles, and of course their own five children. Knox, the oldest, had taken it upon himself to make sure that this occasion was second to none. He and his siblings—except the baby girl, Rainey, who was still in college—contributed financially to reserve the Country Club ballroom, secure one of the most sought-after soul food caterers, and book a live band with a reputation for keeping any party alive with classic and contemporary gospel hits.

Their parents deserved the best.

The only part of the evening that Knox hadn't planned for was the pounding rain. It took a few minutes for the hems of their evening gowns and slacks to dry out, but once they got settled inside the beautifully decorated room, there were no complaints. It had been a wonderful evening.

The wait staff had begun the clean-up and the guests were starting to leave since the storm was finished running its course. Knox was tired. More tired than just about everyone else since he'd been the master planner.

This was the last time he'd do something like this without hiring help.

Actually, when the idea to have a thirty-fifth anniversary celebration was being tossed around, Knox thought he'd have some help, in the form of a wife. Dominique.

"Baby, I'll call the Country Club. We have to get on their calendar early if we want the date," she had said.

"The Country Club?" Knox had given her the side-eye. Dominique had caviar dreams on a Lit'l Smokies budget.

"Yes. I mean, we can't afford to have *our* reception there, but with your family's help, we can have your parents' anniversary there. It will be the talk of the town *and* the church."

Knox felt his stomach tighten. Every time Dominique reminded him that he wasn't yet making quite enough money for her tastes, it was like a blow to his manhood. Being a veterinarian kept him far from the poorhouse, but he was nowhere near the penthouse. That would take time. Ambition. Darn-near a political campaign to rise from a regular staff member to chief of staff, then medical director or regional medical director. Those vets at the top of Mayfield Pet Hospitals were well into six-figures.

If the doors didn't open up at Mayfield, Knox would spread his entrepreneurial wings, start a private practice, and create products to sell in pet stores. All it took was the phrase "created by a veterinarian" for consumers to put faith and a few more dollars into a bag of high-quality dog food.

Better days were coming, that was for sure. But Dominique had to be patient for now. After four years of undergrad, four years of vet school, and a year's residency, Knox had only been in practice two years. Still paying back student loans. Still learning the kinds of things that only experience could provide. He knew this.

Yet, Dominique's underhanded comments about what they couldn't afford, Knox second-guess himself. Am I really as gifted and good as everyone says I am, or are they all lying to me? Am I lying to myself? When will the other shoe drop?

"Oh come on, Knox-y. For me?" She cooed, running a hand under his chin.

Her touch alone convinced him that he needed to do whatever possible to please this woman. She was beautiful. Smelled like roses. Hair long and luxurious, with a smile that charged him from the inside out. She could be bossy sometimes, but Knox could live with it. No one's perfect.

He had acquiesced, easing back onto the sofa, feeling her soft flesh against his back and reveling in the moment. "I'll call my brothers and calculate a budget."

"Knox. This is their *thirty-fifth* anniversary. Throw caution to the wind for once. Stop letting money determine what you'll do. Determine what you want to do first, and then find a way to make it happen." She spouted her financial philosophy into his ear.

When he repeated it to his brothers, Braxton, Jarvis, and West a week later over dinner, they had looked at him like he was crazy.

"Sounds like the broke-folks'-anthem to me," Jarvis

renounced. "I say we talk to Uncle Bush about having it at his house."

"We're always using Uncle Bush's house."

"Because it's amazing," West said.

"And it's free," Braxton noted with a nod.

"Since when are Stoneworths cheap?" Knox asked.

"Since when do Stoneworths try to impress people?" Jarvis quipped. "There's nothing magic about a Country Club. This celebration is about family. God. Food. Fun. All four can be had at Uncle Bush's or even Uncle Hiro's with ease and class."

"Mom and Dad would probably feel better with family, anyway," Braxton seconded.

What they didn't know was that Knox had already reserved the Country Club and paid the nonrefundable deposit upon his future-wife's advice.

Three years, two big family arguments, and one terrible dumped-at-the-altar breakup later, Knox could only thank God for how well this party turned out. He'd thought of throwing in the towel several times, partly because he had made his brothers angry, mostly because he never thought he'd be attending this party alone, without Dominique.

But, prayerfully, he and the fellows got past their differences. Knox regrouped. And tonight, seeing all the love in his parents' eyes as they professed their devotion and adoration for one another at the head table, Knox knew that all the struggles had been worth it.

He'd delegated the after-party duties to Braxton and

his fiancé, Tiffany. They were to pay the vendors and make sure the party favors were distributed. Rainey was to gather the gifts and take them back to the house. Jarvis was to whisk his parents to the airport to catch their flight to a Jamaican resort that very night. Their bags were already in his car. West would handle anything else that popped up.

Knox was out. Ready for a long-deserved rest.

He hugged his parents. "I'm out."

"Oh, Knox," his mother singsonged, "Everything was perfect."

"You kids really did it tonight," his father agreed with a most approving smile.

"Thanks. You guys are the best parents we could have asked for," Knox said.

The photographer captured the moment with a flash.

"You got your tickets and passports?" Knox double-checked.

"Right here." His father tapped his chest. "Son. I know you've been rippin' and runnin' all week to get the party together. Job well done. You go get some rest now."

"Will do."

After a round of good-bye hugs with his siblings, family, and friends that were still gathered, Knox jogged to his Jeep Cherokee. Thunder cracked through the sky, illuminating the clouds, which were heavy with the promise of more rain to come.

Glad that he'd found a relatively calm window to

run out and get in his car, Knox wasted no time starting the engine and beginning the twenty-minute drive home. Make that fifteen—he remembered a shortcut. He drove to the back exit of the Country Club and started down a less-traveled but straight-shot road to the main highway.

Already, Knox could hear his bed calling. *Knox! Come back! I miss you! I need you!*

"I need you, too, baby," he spoke out loud, laughing to himself, thinking that he must be delirious with exhaustion.

He passed a car in the ditch with its lights flashing. Briefly, he glanced inside and noticed there were no passengers inside. *Must have already gotten help.* He was thankful on behalf of whoever that person was because tonight would have been a terrible night to be stranded on this side of this dark road.

The steady beat of his windshield wipers threatened to lull him into a trance, so he turned on the CD player and refreshed himself with some old school gospel. Rance Allen was more his father's speed; however, Knox was quickly starting to develop an appreciation for real music. Must be getting old.

A minute later, Knox squinted as he saw a woman's figure walking along the side of the road. She carried two bags, one on either arm. His heart leapt. *Rainey?* No. It couldn't be Rainey. She was still at the party with her weird-acting boyfriend, Elvin, who had better not *ever* let Rainey walk outside in the rain.

Knox's foot instinctively pressed on the brake. The

woman's rain-soaked pants and a hooded shirt clung to curves Knox would have to ignore for now.

As he got closer, the doctor in him observed a slight limp in her gait.

He slowed even more, matching her pace as he approached her.

She scooted closer to the grass, perhaps to let him pass.

Knox turned off the music and rolled down the passenger's window. Rain came pouring into the car. "Hello!" he yelled to her.

She motioned for him to drive on.

"Are you okay?"

Her brown face flashed at him momentarily from beneath a hoodie. With the rain pounding, he couldn't get a clear view of her features. He did, however, see the gash above her left eye.

"Hello!" he called again.

"Go away!"

Still crawling along beside her in his vehicle, Knox began to assess the situation medically. This woman was walking around in the dark with a limp and a gash. She must have been the woman whose car crashed in the ditch a mile back. Perhaps she'd hit her head in the accident and become disoriented. Confused. In shock.

"Ma'am, I'm a doctor. Would you please get inside?" Never mind what *kind* of doctor he was right now.

She kept walking. Faster.

Knox couldn't leave her like this, but he couldn't

kidnap her either. And the interior of his passenger's side would be soaked if he talked to her like this for the next three miles.

He yelled again, "I'm going to call the police."

She froze. "No!"

"Then how can I help you?"

"You don't have to help me."

That's where she was wrong. If he called himself a man of God, called himself a Stoneworth, called himself a human being and had rescued animals on the side of the road, there was no way Knox would leave an injured woman walking outside in the pouring rain. Even though she wasn't his sister as he'd first fathomed, she was *somebody's* sister. Somebody's daughter. Somebody's something.

"I'm calling 9-1-1."

"No!" She grabbed the door's handle.

Knox slammed on his brakes, unlocked the car and let her in. Truth was, he'd almost been frightened by her sudden change of heart.

She dropped her bags at her feet.

They sat in silence for a few seconds after Knox raised the window from his console pad.

He heard her raspy, shallow breaths. She was afraid. Any woman would be, under the circumstances.

He turned the air conditioner on heat, a gesture he hoped she would receive without another near-argument.

"Where to?"

"You tell me—you're the hero who insists on

saving me," she smarted off, still hiding her face beneath the hood.

"I'm no hero. I'm only trying to help," Knox stated for the record. Despite the darkness, he could see the whites of her fearful eyes staring back at him.

She removed her hood. The outline of her batch of wild, natural curls sprung up in its place.

Initially, Knox activated the overhead light in order to explore the cut and give her his assessment of her wound. But he found himself tongue-tied and staring, instead, at her soft brown eyes, heart-shaped face, the cupid's bow at the top of her full lips, and radiant glow of her rain-slick mocha skin. This was one beautiful woman.

Chapter 2

Jada Jones wasn't ready. All the air flew right out of her chest when he switched on the light and she beheld the stranger's rich brown skin, chiseled nose and chin, immaculate goatee, dark eyes, and smooth lips. *Did he star in a movie?*

Jada was no stranger to good-looking men. This one here, though, took the cake. And the ice cream. And the punch.

She had been blessed, or cursed depending on how one looked at it, with the kind of body that inspired money-makin' rap songs and videos. Her curves had come long before she knew how to handle the attention they garnered, which set her at odds with men and their oogling ways. More than once, she'd had to knee somebody in the groin for trying to go further than she wanted.

She hoped this guy wouldn't try anything with her because, at the moment, she didn't have the energy to slay a brother. Plus, she kind of needed a ride to a shelter. Men don't drive well when they can't sit up straight.

"Do you mind if I take a look at the cut?"

How could she say no? Actually, how could she say *anything* with him leaning over the armrest, his hands drawing near? She could feel the warmth of them already. The touch of his fingers against her face sent an unexpected zing through her body. She jumped from both the excitement and the pain.

"Sorry," he said. "Just trying to gage the depth."

"I'm okay," Jada all but whimpered.

He sat back into his seat, taking with him the musky scent of his cologne. "You need stitches."

Jada could hardly focus on the words coming from his amazingly perfect lips. "Huh?"

"I said you need stitches. Which hospital would you like to go to?"

"Oh. I can't go to a hospital. I don't have insurance."

The man's eyes widened, like he'd never heard the term "no insurance" before.

Jada looked out her window, embarrassed by his expression. People like him—whose lives were all perfect, who went around finding women to rescue in their fancy cars and thought everyone had health insurance—got on her nerves.

"How about a 24-hour clinic? They're pretty reasonable, and they take cash," he suggested with a tinge of hopefulness in his voice.

"I don't have enough for that." The words came out bland, but her throat stung with resentment. *He must be one of those book-smart people with no common sense.* If she had a job, she would have insurance. If she had insurance, she wouldn't need a clinic. But since she had neither job nor insurance, she certainly didn't have extra cash lying around for a clinic. *Duh!*

"I'll pay for it," he offered.

"Negative."

Hail pelted hard and fast against the car now.

"Look, a wound like that needs stitches. Otherwise, it'll probably take forever to heal and get infected along the way," he stated matter-of-factly. "Either I pay for the clinic or I'm taking you to the county hospital. The choice is yours."

"Or I could just get out of the car and keep walking."

"In which case I would call for help because that would mean you're delirious," he said.

"Ugh." *Why does my roadside rescuer have to be so logical?* Alerting law enforcement wasn't on her list of things to do.

Jada had spent a lifetime dealing with county healthcare. Her situation wasn't dire, but she just might die waiting for the doggone stitches. "Fine. The clinic."

They rode in silence to a well-lit shopping center a few miles down the highway. The stores had closed by then. The clinic at the corner had six cars in the lot. Jada hoped that five of them belonged to the employees so they wouldn't have to stay long. She could have this procedure done and then...well, the rest could be decided later.

Once parked, the man hopped out of his seat and made a move to her side of the car. *What in the world?*

He was doing it. He was opening the car door for her, just like she'd seen in old movies and television shows.

I know he's a Huxtable now.

Jada stepped out of the SUV, taking both her bags.

She walked with the man toward the clinic doors.

He was tall. Well over six feet. Broad-shouldered, muscular build, with a confident swag in his stride.

Jada knew his type. And she couldn't wait to get away from him.

Once inside, the man took a seat while Jada approached the reception counter. "Hi—"

"Ooh!" the attendant said, staring at Jada's forehead. "I'm glad you're here!"

"Yes," Jada remained composed, "I need to be seen by a physician."

"Definitely. Do you have insurance?"

"No."

"Okay, private pay," she said under her breath.

The phrase "private pay" sounded so exclusive. Almost desirable. *Yeah, right.*

The lady handed Jada a pen and papers secured in a clipboard. "Fill these out and I'll get you back to see a doctor asap."

"Sure. Let me change clothes first."

"No problem. The restroom is to the right." She pointed.

"Thanks."

Jada followed the woman's direction. One good thing about children's backpacks was their tendency to be plastic, thus waterproof. Jada changed into a blue cotton t-shirt and a pair of black yoga pants. Her tennis shoes still sloshed with wetness. The best she could do was remove her socks and shake her shoes until no more water flung out.

She wiped the floor with paper towels and checked

herself in the mirror. *Ew!* The gash had opened up now and was every bit as ugly as the receptionist's reaction.

Jada sat two seats down from her imposing rescuer and completed the forms. When she got to the section requesting information about the "financially responsible party," she glanced up at him. "Um...there's a part you need to complete."

When he looked at her directly, Jada's heart thumped wildly. Her attraction to him was starting to scare her. *I'm gonna fail the mandatory blood pressure check if I keep looking at him.*

She passed the clipboard and pen to him.

He eyed the paper momentarily. "I don't want to be privy to all your personal information."

Jada chuckled. "Trust me, if you tried to benefit by stealing my identity, you'd be sorely disappointed."

He shrugged. "If you say so."

After completing the bottom portion, Jada took the documents from him. She read, "Knox Stoneworth."

"Yep."

"Sounds like a fake name."

"So does Jada Jones."

"Really?"

"Yes. Really." He smirked slightly.

It ought to be illegal for a man to look this good. Jada steadied herself. "Well. Thank you."

"You're welcome."

"You've been very kind to me, Knox Stoneworth," she said, placing air-quotes around his name. Jada didn't give him time to respond. She returned the papers to the receptionist and waited there for a few moments before the woman buzzed her past the door separating lobby from patient rooms.

The first stop was a scale. Jada weighed 140. She wasn't surprised, though. She knew she'd been losing weight since she lost her job two months earlier and had to move in with her sister, Samyra—affectionately known as Sam. Not that her sister wouldn't or couldn't feed her. Jada simply didn't want to be a burden on Sam and her husband, Patrick. With a one-year-old baby in the house and living on Patrick's police officer salary alone, Jada had known things would be tight, though Sam never complained.

What Jada hadn't known was what kind of foolishness her sister had married into until Jada moved in with them. To put it mildly, Patrick was abusive. In every sense of the word. Emotionally, physically, financially…ridiculously!

Both Sam and Patrick had done a decent job of hiding the physical abuse. Sure, they argued about money, the baby, and everything else Jada imagined married people fussed over. Jada could remember her own parents arguing when she was a little girl, though not quite as heatedly as Sam and Patrick.

Jada stayed out of her sister and brother-in-law's arguments, which always started off small—Sam leaving a baby bottle in the den or Patrick coming home ten minutes later than he'd promised. The spikes in their voices were Jada's cue to grab a novel, put on her headset, and ride it out in her self-created peace…until this evening.

The emergency physician, who introduced herself as Dr. Ashe, concurred with Knox's assessment and prepared Jada for stitches with Betadine and Lidocaine. A second woman whose nametag read "Lisa" entered the treatment room for assistance.

"This won't take long," Dr. Ashe said.

Jada tried her best to relax as she lay flat, waiting for a surgical needle and thread to be forced through her skin. She'd suffered a broken bone from jumping out off a swing once, but never had stitches before.

Suddenly, Jada was scared. What if they messed up and hit a vein? What if the vein they squashed was the one that supplied oxygen to her optical nerves—would she go blind in one eye? Would she have to wear an eye patch and look like a pirate for the rest of her life?

She needed someone there to make sure nothing went wrong. "Umm…would it be possible for my…acquaintance to be here during the procedure?"

"Sure," Dr. Ashe quickly agreed. She motioned for Lisa to go get Knox.

Jada added, "He's a doctor, too." That ought to scare her into doing her best.

"Really? What's his name?"

"Knox Stoneworth."

"Hmm…never heard that name before. Sounds like one I'd remember."

"Yeah. Well, he *is*."

Shortly thereafter, Knox entered the room. His towering frame cast a shadow of relief over her body.

"Hello," Dr. Ashe said from her side of the table. "I hear you're a doctor, too?"

"Yes. A Veterinarian."

Jada bit her tongue. A veterinarian? What?

"Awesome! I seriously considered working with animals. Probably a lot less stressful." Dr. Ashe chuckled.

"I'm sure."

"You work at Mayfield or are you independent?"

"Mayfield for now," Knox said. "Considering my options for the future."

Relieved that Dr. Ashe regarded Knox's profession highly, Jada had to put herself in check. *Give the brother some credit.* Whatever degree Knox had, it was beyond the associate's degree she'd earned. He probably had more letters behind his name than most people.

"We'll be finished up in just a minute," Dr. Ashe said as her assistant laid tools on the silver tray.

Knox looked at Jada again with a raised eyebrow. She read his silent inquiry—*Are you all right?*

She grinned slightly in response—*I'm fine.*

Jada settled into the long chair and waited for the procedure to begin. She closed her eyes, thinking about what a crazy day this had been. Today's dose of trouble at Sam's house had started with another miniscule argument. Another headset time-out for Jada, until she physically felt a thump while sitting in bed. She'd taken off the headset. *Was that thunder from the storm?* She listened. Heard *and* felt the thump, followed by her sister's screams. "No! Don't!"

Jada rushed from her bed and burst into the master suite, where she'd found Patrick restraining Sam in a move Jada had only seen on bad cop shows—perpetrator face-down on the floor, officer with one knee in the perp's back, the downed person's wrists retrained by the officer's bare hands.

Without a word, Jada jumped on Patrick's back and began pounding him with her fists until he let go of Sam.

"Get off me!" he hollered like a five-year-old girl.

Jada dropped to the floor. She picked up a lamp from their dresser and threw it at him. She missed. The shattering glass ricocheted back at her, cutting her deeply above the eyebrow.

Jada touched the fresh wound. Blood covered her fingertips, though she barely felt any pain due to the adrenaline rush.

"You got exactly what you deserve! Stay out of our business!" Patrick yelled as he stormed out of the room.

Sam struggled to catch her breath. "Jada. Stop." She croaked.

"Me? You want *me* to stop? What about *him*?"

"It's not what you think."

Jada stopped for a moment to process those words. "Umm…were you two flirting just now?"

"It's…we had an argument. That's all."

Blood dripped into Jada's eye. She swiped it away. She watched her sister slowly come to a standing position.

"You're hurt," Sam said, raising a hand to Jada's face.

Jada slapped her hand away. "I know what I saw. Patrick was *hurting* you. And not just with words this time. I'm calling the police."

"Shhhhh!" Sam bit her bottom lip. "Don't bother. He works for them, remember? This is a nice little suburban department. Officers work here because they don't want to be around trouble. They're close-knit. They won't do anything to rock the boat."

She spoke like she'd already been down that dead-end road before.

The front door slammed. Patrick was gone.

With the immediate threat gone from out of the house, Jada thought perhaps she could talk some sense into her sister. "You don't have to live like—"

"*You* don't know anything! You're not married! You don't have kids! You don't know what it's like to be in my shoes," Sam cried, her eyes wild with desperation.

Sam crammed her feet into a pair of shaggy house shoes. She pulled a coat from the closet. "I have to follow him. Stay here with the baby. Give me your keys."

"That would be a no. Have you lost your mind? Why are you chasing someone who just tried to kill you?"

"Jada, I need your keys. I'm trying to save my family here."

"If this is your definition of family, it's not worth

saving!"

Sam shifted her weight to one side. "Are you going to give me your keys or not?"

"Not."

A charged silence held between them as they stared-off.

"Then get out," Sam ordered.

"Gladly."

With that, Jada grabbed her purse and stuffed one of her nephew's spare backpacks with everything she might need for the next few days. If she knew her sister, Sam would come to her senses in the next day and they'd be packing *Patrick's* bags real soon.

She'd found directions to a cheap hotel and was headed to check-in when her GPS suddenly gave out in the stormy weather. She'd tried to remember the route but realized she'd gotten off track when she passed the Country Club. The winding roads around the golf course, slick streets, the nearly-bald tires on her hooptie combined to create the small disaster in a muddy ditch.

And now here she was in a clinic getting stitches with two doctors in the room, one of which could have graced the cover of a *GQ* magazine.

"All finished," Dr. Ashe announced. "Lisa will give you the follow-up paperwork at the front desk." She snapped off her gloves and tossed them in the step trash. "It was nice meeting you, Dr. Stoneworth."

"Same here."

They were able to shake hands now.

Jada sat upright and prepared to hop down from the

chair.

Knox gripped her hand.

Jada sucked in a ball of air.

"Just trying to help you get down," he explained himself.

She knew exactly what he was doing. It was the pleasure of his soft, warm hands that snatched her wits away. "Thank you."

When Lisa presented Jada with aftercare instructions and the bill, Jada's nose twitched— *$345.28!*

Knox had already whipped out his credit card.

"Hold up," Jada said, fishing through her purse for her wallet. She gave Lisa her last bit of cash. "Apply this first."

"Certainly." Lisa counted the money, tapped a few keys on her computer, then said, "That brings it down to two seventy-three twenty-eight."

Knox didn't hesitate to pass his credit card across the counter.

Jada watched as the plastic was swiped through the digital reader.

What if it doesn't go through? What if he's been lying to me all along?

A strip of white paper came jutting from the top of the machine. "If you'll sign right above your name."

He took the pen Lisa offered him.

Jada stole a glance at the paper to confirm his name. There it was in plain black-and-white. *Knox Stoneworth.*

He gave the slip to Lisa, who exchanged the signed one for a second strip, a receipt.

"Have a nice evening," Lisa said.

Jada and Knox returned the salutation.

They walked back to his car. The rain had slacked to a light mist.

Once again, he opened the door for her. "Thank you."

He tipped his head gently and closed it before walking to his side and entering.

"Thank you," Jada gushed with gratitude, "for everything."

"No problem."

She wondered if he was going to drop the bomb now, ask her to spend the night with him. Or maybe he was married and he was about to offer a side-chick proposition. Of course, she'd turn down both offers. Then he'd lock the doors, peal out of the parking lot, put the pedal to the medal, and kidnap her! Then she'd just have to jump out of a moving car and scrape her face...wait... that scenario made no sense since he'd just paid close to three hundred dollars for her stitches.

"Where to?" he asked.

Jada reeled her imagination back from the high-speed jump-out. "Huh?"

"Where would you like me to take you?"

Good question. Jada had used all her money at the clinic. She honestly didn't have an answer.

Knox shrugged. "I suppose you could stay at my—" *Here it comes!* Jada thought—"parents' pool house."

Not exactly what she had in mind. "Your what?"

"My parents have a pool house. They usually have someone there—a guest minister, a family member in transition—but it's empty now."

Wooo hoo. Your parents have a pool house. Must be nice. "No, thank you. I'll just...you can take me to the gas station. I can take it from there. But thanks for everything. You've got some good Karma coming to you."

He laughed slightly. "I don't believe in Karma. What I *do* believe is that you need a place to stay for the night. Am I correct?"

Jada smacked her lips. "Look, I'm from the *hood*, okay? I know how to survive on the streets."

"Really?"

"Yes."

"Says the woman with a 'Bob the Builder' backpack?" He pointed toward the footboard.

There, staring up at them, was the screen print of her nephew's favorite person in the whole wide world, besides his mom.

Jada took a deep breath. Knox was right. She had nowhere to go, no way to get there, and no street creds with Bob on her back. "Well...as long as the house is empty."

"It is."

"And you're not staying there?"

He raised his hands in a gesture of innocence. "No, ma'am."

"And you won't try anything?"

He raised his hands higher. "Promise. I'll stay in the main house."

Jada would have to be plain ignorant not to know by now that she was in the midst of a true gentleman. "Okay."

Somehow, this Knox Stoneworth was inching his way into her jacked-up world.

Chapter 3

Knox had to be totally honest with himself and God. Had Jada been unattractive, greedy, and/or genuinely mean, he would have dropped her off at the clinic and wished her well. Jada, however, had proven herself none of those things in less than two hours.

When he finally got to see her head-on, in full light at the clinic, Knox couldn't believe his good fortune. He'd even asked himself if maybe he was being punked. How many times does a man drive up on a beautiful woman walking down a street? Let alone a beautiful woman with spunk and quick wit who had an inner moral compass that prevented her from taking advantage of his kindness?

Knox exited the freeway and made the familiar journey to his parents' house. The wide streets, mature trees, and automatic lighting systems in the neighborhood gave glimpses of his family's financial blessing.

"Nice zip code," Jada commented.

"Thanks."

"Your parents doctors, too?"

"No." He couldn't really tell the whole story in such a short time. "My dad played in the N-F-L for a while."

"Oh." Her voice rang with understanding. "Gotcha."

Knox parked his Jeep under the porte cochere, the half-way point between the main house and the pool house. The pool sparkled from the overhead lights leading to the basketball court further down the property's cobblestone walkway.

"We're here."

"I see."

Jada got out before he had the chance to help her.

He walked her to the pool house and opened the door. "We don't usually keep it locked. But, of course, you can lock it while you're inside tonight."

"Why don't you keep it locked?" she asked, stepping across the threshold.

"I don't know. Never really thought about it." Knox turned on the lights. Except for the bathroom, every section of the house was visible at a glance. Kitchen area and dining table to the right. Living area with sofa sleeper, fireplace and television to the left, office nook straight ahead.

His mother had decorated the small house in gray and white with placid blue touches, keeping it neutral so that her guests wouldn't feel overwhelmed by her personal tastes.

"This is nice, Knox. Thank you. Again."

Hearing Jada speak his name was all the reward he needed. Her hair was starting to dry, creating soft tendrils around her temples. Jada was a perfect picture of black beauty—thick lips, kinky hair, almond-shaped eyes, and an aura of confidence he couldn't put into words. She had the kind of beauty he probably couldn't have appreciated without an understanding of his heritage.

If she shared the same faith, she'd make an

unbelievable package.

"I can take your wet clothes inside the main house and dry them for you, if you'd like."

"That would be great."

He hadn't expected her to accept his kindness so quickly, but he was glad for it.

She unzipped the backpack a little too far. Out tumbled hair potions, a toothbrush, and some other feminine products Knox had no desire to witness.

He turned his head sharply, shielding his vision with his hand. "I'm so sorry."

Jada giggled. "Sorry for what?"

"I didn't mean to see your...personal effects."

"Haven't you ever lived in a house with a woman?" Jada bent down to pick up the objects.

"My mom. My little sister. They kept all their stuff far from me and my three brothers, and we were grateful."

Jada inquired, "You've never lived with a girlfriend?"

"No."

From his peripheral vision, Knox could see that Jada was finished handling her lady-items.

He took the wet clothes from her now.

Jada's eyes narrowed hard at him.

"What?"

"Are you serious? How old are you?"

"Thirty-one next month."

"And you've *never* lived with a woman?" she quizzed.

"No. Why is that so hard to believe?"

Before he knew what was happening, Knox felt a sting on his arm. Jada had pinched him.

"Ow!"

"Are you real?"

"Of course I'm real." He rubbed the spot like it hurt, though it would take a lot more than a little pinch to do damage to his biceps.

"Well let me pinch *myself*, then, because I've never met a man my age or over who hadn't spent at least a few weeks or months living with his girl." Jada stopped, her eyes calculating. "Unless he lived with his mother."

"I don't live with my mother. I've never lived with a woman. And have no idea how old you are or who you know, so I cannot respond intelligently to your observation. Is there a problem?" The question came out more sharply than he'd intended. He'd had enough of her attitude.

Jada blinked slowly. She pulled at one of her hair's coils. "I'm sorry. You've been nothing but nice to me all evening. I just…I've never met anyone like you."

Their eyes locked in a gentle, unspoken truce.

Knox nodded acceptance of her apology and decided to offer an explanation he hoped—*prayed*—she would understand. "It might help to let you know that I'm a believer."

"A believer of what?"

"Jesus Christ. He makes me who I am. I'm not saying I'm perfect—"

"I know. Nobody is," she cut him off. Then a smile spread across her face and she said in nearly a whisper, "I know Jesus, too. Not for long." She bit her lip. "I think it's pretty amazing to see Him in you."

Knox could have kissed her full lips right then and there. Probably wouldn't have been very Jesus-like, however. "Goodnight, Jada."

"Goodnight."

Knox nearly ran back to the main house with Jada's wet clothes in hand. He had to get out of there before something he didn't want to happen happened. No less with a woman he'd just met. Scary sometimes how quickly his body reminded him that despite his close relationship with Christ, he was made of flesh.

He unlocked the side door of the main house and called, "Hello!" so as not to scare his sister.

She didn't answer.

He walked past the laundry room and into the kitchen. "Rainey? You here?"

The sound of his voice bounced off the stainless steel pots and pans hanging from the rack above the island. Still no answer.

He checked his phone. *Twelve forty-two.* Knox dialed his little sister's number, a lecture ready to roll off his tongue.

"Hello?"

"Rainey, where are you?"

"I'm coming in the door."

He looked over his shoulder and saw the knob turning. He set his phone and Jada's clothes on the

33

counter, crossed his arms, and watched as Rainey, with her long flowing hair and form-fitting dress, waltzed past the door looking like a grown woman.

Rainey gave him a giant hug. "Great party, Knox. Mom and Dad were so proud." She kicked off her too-tall-to-be-my-little-sister heels, then picked them up off the floor.

"Yeah. But where have you been?"

"I took Elvin back to his hotel. And now I'm home. So glad to be here." Her sweet voice vibrated against his chest.

"What time did you leave the party?"

She raised up. "Why?"

"Because it doesn't take two hours to drop Elvin off at a hotel and make it back here."

"Wait." She stepped away from him. "Why aren't you at your place anyway? Did Dad send you to spy on me and make sure I wasn't staying in Elvin's hotel room?"

"No. But you didn't answer my question. What took you so long to get back home?"

"I don't intend to answer your question," she snapped. She walked to the refrigerator and grabbed a bottle of water. "I'm twenty-four years old. You all need to stop treating me like a child."

Knox exhaled. How could he not treat her like a child when she was six years younger than him? When she'd begged him to teacher her to tie her shoes? When he'd snuck into her room and added extra money to the tooth fairy's stash? Like it or not, Rainey would always be Knox, Braxton, Jarvis, and West Stoneworth's little sister.

"Is there a reason I *should* be spying on you?"

She gulped down some of the water, twisted the top back on, and set the bottle on the counter. "Look, Knox. You're the oldest. Everyone looks up to you. You, my dear brother, are perfectly poised to alert this entire family that Rainey Elizabeth Stoneworth is now an adult. So I'm going to say this to you one time and one time only. Anything I've had the desire to do has already been done at least once during the six years I've been away at college. Can you please send the memo to your brothers and your parents?"

If Knox could have covered his ears and screamed "La-la-la-la-la!" he would have. He reminded himself, *I'm the big brother here.* "We all want what's best for you."

Rainey spotted the clothes on the counter. "What's this?"

Knox grabbed Jada's belongings. "Clothes."

Rainey quickly snatched Jada's shirt from Knox's arms. She held it in the air. Examined the garment. "Medium. Babydoll cut. Not your size or your cut, Knox."

"They belong to a friend. I'm washing and drying them for her."

She tossed the shirt back to him. Her chin lowered as she glared up at him. "Where is she?"

"She's in the pool house."

"And why is she in the pool house instead of *her*

house?"

"It's a long story."

"I bet it is." Now it was Rainey's turn to cross her arms. "I'm listening."

"Look. It's late—"

"Oh!" She threw her hands in the air. "Suddenly, it's too *late* for talkin' since we're talkin' about *you* instead of *me*!"

Knox shook his head. "It's not what you're thinking."

"So explain to me how it's not a double-standard that Dad allowed Jarvis's girlfriend to stay in the pool house the whole week of Spring Break when he was a sophomore in undergrad, but my boyfriend can't stay a weekend and I'm working on a Ph.D.?"

His sister was wiser and much more outspoken than he remembered. "I can't speak for Dad. I can only speak for myself. The woman in the pool house is *not* my girlfriend."

"I find no comfort in that admission, Knox. Exactly what is your relationship to the woman for whom you have afforded temporary residence in our parents' pool house?"

Knox hated it when Rainey went "Victorian" on him. She'd been reading one too many novels in school. "Rainey—"

"Perhaps *I* should be spying on *you*."

"Enough with the old English, all right? I'm not here to spy on you."

Her face softened slightly as her shoulders slumped

in concession. "I believe you, Knox."

"It's just...man, Rainey, you grew up so fast." He put the clothes down again and drew his sister into a hug. "Here you are now. Beautiful. Brilliant—"

"And don't forget blessed to have been raised by parents who taught me right from wrong. You guys have to trust that now," she said. "I'm going to make my mistakes. God knows I watched my brothers make plenty."

"Truly. But, you know, men...we don't see your personality or your brain first. We see the outside, initially. I mean, if you weren't my sister, I'd be tryna holla."

She stared up at him and cheesed the kid-smile he wished he could frame. "I couldn't be with a guy like you, Knox. You're way too serious."

"What's wrong with me?"

Rainey slipped out of his embrace. "There's nothing wrong with you. We're too much alike."

Knox chuckled. Yep, Rainey is much wiser now.

Rainey yawned. "Goodnight, big bro."

"Night."

He watched his little sister clunk up the staircase to her room lamenting the fact that one day, probably sooner than later, his father would be giving Rainey away to somebody. Whoever he was had better be legit or he'd have to deal with the Stoneworth men.

Knox scooped up Jada's clothes and walked across the main foyer, two living areas—one formal, one informal—and finally to the washroom. Since Jada's clothes were dark and cotton, he threw them in the wash at once, adding a dash of powder.

It dawned on him that he had no other clothes for himself. West might have a few things left in his room, but they were bound to be too small. His father's clothes would be too wide. Knox would have to rough it until the morning.

He parked himself on the chaise in the casual family room and turned the television to ESPN to catch up on the day's sports activity. One glance at Serena Williams reminded Knox of the woman in the pool house. Brown. Curvy. Self-assured.

His phone pulsed in his pocket. Curiosity about his late-night caller turned to annoyance when he saw the name on the screen. Dominique.

"Hello," he answered.

"Hey, Knox, sorry to call at this hour."

She paused.

He waited for her explanation.

"What do you need, Dominique?"

"Can I get a *how are you*? Obviously, something is wrong if I'm calling you this late."

Whatever was wrong in Dominique's life had nothing to do with him. He cleared his throat. She'd have to continue without his response.

"Well, I was on the computer a minute ago. Got an alert on my email about a charge to the old joint credit card. You went to an urgent care clinic?"

Knox reached for his wallet and tabbed through the cards. In an instant, he realized that he'd pulled the wrong card at the clinic. "My bad. I'll pay the charged amount first thing in the morning."

"Is everything all right? Are you hurt?"

"No. It was for a friend."

"Oh."

Knox almost wished Dominique would ask him more questions so he could let her know that he was in the company of another woman; give the appearance that he'd moved on with his life.

"Is your…*friend* okay?"

He couldn't have asked for a better segue. "Yes, she's fine."

"*She?*"

"Yes. She." Dreams do come true.

He heard Dominique's lips smack softly. "That's good."

He'd had enough fun at Dominique's expense. "Like I said, I'll resolve this in the morning."

"Will you call me when you've taken care of it?" she asked.

"No. You should be able to see it online."

"Yeah, I guess so. Goodnight, Knox. I'm glad you're okay."

"Night, Dominique."

Knox didn't want to give her any reason to call him again. He tapped and typed his way to the payment screen and cleared up the matter immediately. This account, which Dominique had opened in both their names without his permission and a little forgery when they were planning for the wedding, was their last connection.

He'd found out about the account during mediation, which Dominique had agreed to instead of a lawsuit for sticking him and his family with most of the bills for a wedding that she literally walked out of. As the bills rolled in, Dominique admitted to the mediator that she'd gotten "caught up" in her desire to throw an extravagant ceremony and impress her friends, family, co-workers, and sorority sisters. None of whom were there for her when she'd been ordered to pay 80 percent of the wedding expenses except for the ring, which she had to return outright to Knox.

Thankful to have found out what kind of person Dominique truly was before saying "I do," Knox had paid his portion in the first six months. Two years later, Dominique and the dude she'd married were still making payments on their end.

Knox checked the remaining balance. Less than two thousand dollars. He should be free and clear of Dominique soon. *Thank God.*

He propped the throw pillow underneath his neck and got comfortable. His mind drifted back to Dominique and their 18-month courtship. He had met her at a funeral, of all places. One of his father's old teammates passed away. His father had just undergone cataract surgery, so he couldn't drive to the ceremony. Knox had done the honor of taking him and been "rewarded" by meeting the deceased man's great niece, Dominique Wellington.

She gave a charming speech on behalf of the

"greats" in their family. "Uncle Dallas gave us kids five dollars every time we saw him. And what would he say?" She'd waited for the audience to gear up, and several of them laughed along with her as she repeated his words. "Don't pick the wrong horse." Those gathered had laughed, Knox included.

He appreciated Dominique's height, her slender build, and the way her honey-blond spikes accented her angular face. But perhaps most importantly, he liked the fact that, like him, she seemed to have a strong connection with her family. In the past, some of his girlfriends had been turned off by the fact that he and his family were so close.

"It's just weird," his ex, Tamara, had told him. "I see my mom and dad, like, twice a year. You guys see each other every other week or so. And you talk on the phone to your brothers like they're your best friends."

"They are," he had agreed.

Tamara shook her head. "That's crazy to me. I was taught that when you grow up, you *leave* the nest. You get out there and make it on your own."

Knox couldn't have disagreed more. "How can you be part of a village if you leave?"

"Easy. When you're finished being raised by the village, you bounce."

"Then who stays in the village for the next generation?"

Tamara shrugged. "I don't know. That's a Stoneworth issue."

And she would never be one, with that attitude.

Michelle Stimpson

Dominique, however, had sisters, brothers, cousins, aunts, uncles, grands—people who loved her and welcomed Knox into their presence. And his family had been delighted to embrace her.

There had been a few warning signs that Dominique was too materialistic and manipulative along the way to the altar—little "white," exaggerated lies to her sisters about how much she'd spent on a purse or a pair of shoes, insisting that Knox be dressed a certain way when they went to her mom's house. Jarvis had even said something to Knox once about Dominique's motives. Of course, Knox told Jarvis to mind his own business.

But in the end, Jarvis had been right.

How could I have been so blind?

He'd been wrong about a woman once before. Jumped in with his whole heart. Overlooked the warning signs and loved her beyond her faults. Tried to love her like Christ loves the church.

Where did that get me? Nowhere.

Knox wasn't going to be the same fool twice.

Wait a minute—didn't I just do the same thing tonight? What was I thinking, picking up a woman on the side of the road?

He knocked his forehead with a fist. He had to slow down. No matter how witty and pretty Jada was, he wouldn't be so naïve this time.

Chapter 4

Jada didn't bother pulling out the sofa bed. After taking a shower, she found a blanket and a sheet in the linen closet and curled up on the couch. She protected the light-colored sofa's fabric from her hair with a towel and tried to get some sleep.

Only she couldn't. Not with thoughts of Knox Stoneworth dancing through her head.

Moonlight lit the small house, and her eyes landed on the pictures on the fireplace mantel. She couldn't make out any faces, but there were clearly seven heads in Knox's family portrait.

Jada couldn't relate. She had one sister with the same mother, and one brother with the same father. Never any peace between the parents, thus never a family picture like these Stoneworths.

How many times am I going to say that name in my head?

She was sick of them already with their perfect family and this pool house that was almost bigger than the apartment from which she'd been evicted two months ago in December. Two months before that, in October, she'd received a pink slip in the envelope with her last check at Texas Pipe and Iron Supply Company.

She laughed at the patter forming in her head now. Something significant happened every two months it seemed. In August, the most important thing she'd ever done took place while attending a women's conference with a friend. Jada had heard the gospel of Jesus

Christ—the story of how He came to set people free from sin and exchange lives with him—in a way she'd never heard it before. Well, maybe she'd heard it before, but she'd never actually received the good news in her heart until it burned into her heart that day.

As a gift, the conference host had given her a Bible and plan to read the Bible in a year, starting with 1 John. Shortly thereafter, Jada got the job offer in Texas. She'd jumped at the chance to spread her wings, move outside Memphis, and put her brand new associate's degree in accounting to good use. This would also give her a chance to spend more time with Sam and the baby.

Jada's mother had fussed but, in the end, agreed that a change was good for Jada. "Don't forget, you can always come back home. Long as I'm living, you got a place to stay."

Jada appreciated her mother's loyalty but prayed to God she wouldn't have to take her mother up on the offer.

The first weeks at Texas Pipe and Iron were great. Jada made new acquaintances and thought she was learning the ropes. The ropes, however, turned out to be nooses. The manager over Accounts Payable, a man named Miles Rufus, had some non-standards practices that Jada questioned. The system of checks and balances seemed thwarted, and Jada brought it to everyone's attention in a staff meeting, thinking she was doing the right thing. After all, that's what she'd been taught at Southwest Tennessee Community

College—Communication was the key to smooth and professional business operations.

The follow up to that meeting had come by way of a private meeting with Mr. Rufus himself, who not-so-subtly warned Jada not to overstep her boundaries.

From then on, Jada knew to watch her back. Her law courses were still fresh on her mind. People who committed crimes at her level went to federal prison when convicted. No knocking time off the sentence for good behavior or because Uncle Sam needed space for more felons.

Jada did most of what she was required to do, except sign off on products received from a company named "RRWC." She couldn't find invoices or packing slips—no paper trail whatsoever. When she said something to Miles about it, he'd told her, "Just go ahead and sign off on it. Those shipments arrive at our Houston office, but we pay from Dallas."

"Why doesn't the Houston office handle the payables, then?" she'd asked innocently.

Miles turned away from his computer screen. His eyes hooded with indignation, he said, "Because we handle it *here*. Just forward the RRWC files to me. I'll get McKayla to handle them."

Fine. Less work for me, Jada had thought to herself as she walked away from Miles's office. She had second-guessed herself for a while there, wondering if maybe she should have just followed along. Been a team player. But as she read more of the Bible, she saw herself differently. She'd never been the just-go-along type before she met Christ. She certainly couldn't conform now.

Three weeks later, Jada was fired. With no income and no positive reference from Texas Pipe and Iron, Jada lost her apartment and was forced to move in with Sam and Patrick.

A lot of good her personal principles and Christian standards had done her so far.

"God," she whispered, "I know You can hear me. And I know You love me. I need to see You in my life. And please help my sister. What Patrick did to her...well, You know. I just...need a break. Amen."

She closed her eyes. Seconds later, she added a note to the prayer. "And thank You for sending Knox to help me tonight. Please bless him, although I don't know what else he could possibly need since he and his family already have everything. Amen again."

***

The pool house brightened with the first rays of sunlight, waking Jada much earlier than she'd planned. She figured out how to turn on the television hoping to catch a home and garden show. Her stomach, however, had other ideas.

In the quaint kitchen, she surveyed the available ingredients and surmised that she had everything needed to make pancakes and a side of scrambled eggs with cheese. She created her own syrup for the pancakes using jelly, cornstarch, and water since she couldn't find a bottle of maple in the pantry.

Knock-knock.

Jada washed her hands in the dishwater and walked toward the door. Knox's tall frame was outlined in the curtains. She opened the door to a vision of hunkified man even more attractive in the natural sunlight. "Good morning."

"Morning." He held a white sack in on hand and her neatly folded clothes in the other. "I got you some doughnuts, but it smells like you've got something better already."

"Pancakes and eggs," she said.

"Smells great."

"Have some?" she offered, stepping aside to let him in.

"Don't mind if I do."

He placed the clothes on the arm of the couch and sat at the oak table as Jada prepared his plate.

"No problems with the sutures last night?"

"None. Thanks for asking." She gave him a pancake and a half, since she'd prepared three, and split the eggs down the middle. She poured him a glass of apple juice and joined him at the table.

"This looks delicious. Was there pancake mix in the pantry?" he asked.

"*Pancake* mix?" Jada scorned.

"Yeah. Aunt Jemima? Bisquick?"

She shook her head. "No. There was no boxed mix. I made it from scratch."

"Really?"

"Yes. I'm from the hood, remember? I know how to make do with whatever I have."

"This looks like way more than *do*." Knox smiled, obviously impressed. "Can't wait to taste them." He held out his hands. "Grace?"

Jada slipped her hands into the smooth groove of his hands.

"Father, thank You for this food we are about to receive. Let it be nourishment to our bodies. And bless the hands that prepared it. Amen."

He gave Jada's hands a squeeze.

"Amen," she agreed, wondering how in earth she was going to regain use of these tingling hands of hers. She rubbed them against her thighs.

Knox took a bite of pancake. His face screwed up. He closed his eyes, opened them, and peered at her. "Jada. You just changed my life."

"What?" She sniggered.

"I hereby swear off all pancake mixes for the rest of my life. And what kind of syrup is this?"

"Made if from jelly."

"What do you call it?" he asked.

"Umm...syrup made from jelly," Jada answered. She watched in amusement at Knox all but inhaled the pancakes. Poor guy. Probably living alone in his massive apartment, surviving on fast food and frozen entrees.

She was glad to be able to turn the tables and give him something, for once. "You want more?"

"Do you mind?"

"No. It's the least I can do." Jada finished the last few bites of hers and quickly whipped up another batch of batter, enough for two more man-sized pancakes.

"You sleep well?" he asked.

"Yes, thank you."

"I called a friend. A mechanic. He towed your car to his shop. He says he'll give you an estimate Monday on repairs. He's very reasonable."

Jada focused on the edges of the pancakes, waiting for them to take form. "Tell him not to bother. I only had liability, and I can't pay to get it fixed right now. Car's older than dirt anyway. He can scrap it and keep the money. Should cover the towing fee, I'm guessing."

Knox shrugged. "Cool. I just didn't want the city to tow it—they'd charge a daily impound fee on top of towing."

"Thanks for taking care of it." Jada flipped the pancakes. This whole scenario was unreal. Her in the kitchen cooking. A man sitting at the table waiting for her to prepare his plate. Pleasant conversation. Peace. In a nice house. All they lacked was a white picket fence. *This is surreal.*

I

Chapter 5

Knox wanted to join Jada at the stove, maybe even help her in some way. He didn't want to come on too strong, though.

He thought of asking her to give him the recipe for the pancakes, but as he watched her make the batter, he realized she didn't have a recipe; it was a pinch of this, a dash of that, and an egg. She'd added a little more flour to thicken the batter and voila, he had a second helping of heaven.

She joined him again at the table.

He sopped up a corner with syrup and chewed the fluffy hotcake. "You oughta sell this stuff."

"It's not that serious."

"I respectfully disagree."

A knock at the door got both their attention. *Rainey*.

"Who's that?" Jada asked, skepticism written on her face.

"My sister."

Her lips pressed into a fine line. "Your *real* sister or your *play* sister."

Knox ripped a paper towel from the dispenser on the table and wiped his mouth. "I'm too old to have a play *anything*."

Jada leaned to the side. Her eyes swept up and down his body. "Excuse me."

Rainey—wearing pajamas, a bathrobe, and slippers—bum-rushed Jada. "Hello. I'm Rainey Stoneworth, Knox's sister. And you are?"

"Jada Jones. Nice to meet you."

Knox recognized the bratty tone in Rainey's voice.

"Can we help you with something?" Knox finally caught up and asked.

"No. I was just coming by to ask questions, as you and my other brothers did to my friend, Elvin." Rainey turned her attention back to the victim. "So, Jada, how did you meet my brother? Where are you from? What's your occupation? Do you have children? Do they live with you? If not, are you current on child support and where is yo' baby daddy?"

Jada's brown eyes slid up to Knox.

"You don't have to answer her questions," he assured Jada. "Let's go."

"But you guys made Elvin answer *your* questions." Rainey pouted. "It's only fair."

"Well, I don't know why your boyfriend didn't stand up for himself, but I'm not going to answer your questions," Jada insisted. "Not today."

"Mmmph." Rainey huffed. She poked her lips at Knox. "Wonder what would have happened if Elvin had told *you* that. Y'all probably would have kicked him out of the party."

Jada stood. "You don't have to worry about kicking me out. I'm leaving."

Rainey said nothing.

Knox intervened, "Jada, you don't—"

She held up a hand. "No. She's right," Jada said. "Your family has a right to know the people you're involved with—especially since you guys have been hounding her about her boyfriend. But since you and I aren't involved, we can end this whole conversation right here and now."

Jada grabbed the dried clothes and her backpack and went to the bathroom.

Knox spoke to Rainey between gritted teeth. "What are you doing?"

Rainey's eyes were saucers. "I was only kidding. Where's her sense of humor?"

"You need to apologize."

Rainey nodded. "I will. But I need you to understand that this is exactly how I feel when you guys grilled Elvin. Not so great, huh?"

"Men are used to it," Knox defended his examination crew.

Rainey tsked and frowned. "Another double standard. This is sad. What progress have we made as a civilized society?"

"None, all right? Absolutely none." This girl was about to make him call their father.

Jada emerged from the bathroom in fresh clothes. She'd picked her hair out into a classy afro and applied a glossy shine to her lips. "I'm ready to leave now."

Rainey stepped forward. "Listen, Jada, I'm sorry. I didn't mean to upset you."

"I'm not upset. No harm." She hoisted the backpack on her shoulder. "You ready, Knox?"

"Yeah."

"Okay." Rainey tried her airline stewardess smile. "Thanks for coming. See you later."

"I'll be at the car." Jada let herself out of the house.

Knox's eyes narrowed at Rainey. "I hope you haven't messed this up."

"She said you two aren't together. What's there to mess up?"

"I don't know. Yet."

Knox left the house and joined Jada at the vehicle. Once they were inside, he apologized again for Rainey.

Jada repeated herself, "No harm."

"You mean that?"

"Yes," she said.

He didn't know her well enough to determine if this meant "yes" for real or "no, but I'm not ready to discuss it now" or even "no, and I'll tuck this away in my heart until I get really angry, then I'll bring it up again."

With no history, he could only take Jada for her word.

"I'm headed to church. Would you like to come with me?"

"No. I'm still tired. You can take me to my sister's house. She's off twenty and North Main."

Knox started the car, still hoping for a clue about Jada's temperament. Maybe she really was over Rainey's insulting inquiry. If so, he could not let this woman get away. Someone who was honest and genuine? Who didn't play mind games? Top those characteristics with someone who wasn't obsessed with living a lifestyles of the rich and famous—knew how to make whatever she had in her hands work?

"Music?" she requested.

Knox indulged, choosing a fast tune from the latest Jonathan Nelson CD.

She guided him to a newer subdivision. Knox was familiar with the general area of the southern sector of Dallas. The cities in that area were reinventing themselves, securing some of the more popular franchises and bringing new money.

"Turn left on the second street."

The cul-de-sac was filled with kids racing big wheels. Knox smiled as he reminisced. "Man, those were the days!"

"What?"

"Big wheels!"

"Oh. I never had one. Didn't want one, either."

"Serious?"

"Why waste Santa's time on a Big Wheel when you can ask for Beanie Babies instead?"

"Are you talking about those stuffed animals?"

Jada rolled her neck. "Yes. I would go through the fire for one of those."

Shocked, Knox could only laugh. "I wouldn't peg you as the Beanie Baby type."

"There was no type. Anyone could love one. They were soft and cuddly. My mom worked an extra shift to get me one for my eighth birthday. I still have it," she admitted.

Knox looked over at her in disbelief.

"Third house," Jada said.

Knox slowly proceeded down the street as the kids

on Big Wheels dispersed to the sidewalk.

Jada retrieved her belongings from the back seat. "Thank you for everything. I really appreciate it. You're a nice person with a nice family. I wish nothing but the best for you all."

"Same here." Is she leaving me forever?

Jada pulled on the door's handle. "Oh, and one more thing."

Knox could breathe again.

She stated, "Don't forget to tell your friend the mechanic to do whatever he wants with that old clunker."

No! No! No! This could not be happening. Knox stalled, "Is your sister expecting you?"

"Probably. She knows I won't leave her with that maniac husband of hers. If I have to get another six stitches, I won't stand for him to put his hands on her again."

Anger shot through Knox. "Whoa, whoa. Wait a minute. I thought you'd hit your head in the car accident?"

"No. I got cut by glass from a lamp I'd thrown at my brother-in-law after I caught him red-handed."

"Why didn't you call the police?"

"He *is* the police. He works for the department. My sister says they won't do anything to their own."

Knox's mind was a million pieces of confusion. "So your brother-in-law is here?"

"He's probably at work."

"But when he gets off, he'll come here?"

"Yep."

"Is it safe here for you?"

"Please," Jada smacked, "he is *not* going to hit *me*. He'd have to pass through a skillet and some knives to get at me."

Knox's chest pulled with the thought of a man hurting Jada, or any woman for that matter. But especially Jada.

"Don't worry, Knox. I'll be fine. I'm from the hood. I got this." She stepped out of the car.

"Wait." He got out of the car and took the bags from her hand. "Is this...*it*?"

"Yes. I mean...unless you..." she left the ball in his corner.

Knox's heart twisted and turned as he wrestled with the idea of putting his feelings on the line again. What if Jada wasn't as sincere as she seemed? He'd been wrong before. Jumped too soon. What if he were wrong again?

And what if all this stuff with her family was simply how they rolled—drama, drama, and more drama. He didn't have time to be part of a blockbuster movie starring himself.

But what if Jada *was* the one?

He needed to pray.

Knox helped Jada carry the bags to her sister's door. "I'll be praying about this situation between your sister and her husband," he said. It was too soon for major promises.

"Thank you."

Chapter 6

Jada felt the tears stinging at the base of her eyes when Knox walked back to his car. Unlike the hunky man in romance movies, he had not reached for her. He hadn't embraced her and whisked her away from the chaos better known as her life.

She could have smacked herself for allowing herself to feel a little hope with Knox. It could never happen. They were from two different worlds, two different backgrounds. Knox came from a family, a home—a home with a pool house! He had a different way of thinking. His default personality was set to "positive" while hers was set to "reality."

He was a veterinarian, the kind of person people respected instantly.

Can't even make his own pancake mix. She laughed to herself as she repositioned the backpack.

Jada knocked on the door. She saw Patrick's silhouette through the window sheers and cringed.

"It's your sister," she heard him say through the door. His footsteps tapered off as he walked away.

She heard Knox's car still running. *Is he going to say something else?*

To her heart's dismay, Jada's sister opened the door. "Hey."

"Hey. I'm back."

"I see." As Sam focused on Jada's bandage, the sarcasm in her voice disappeared. "Are you all right?"

"Yeah. Got a few stitches."

Sam stepped aside, allowing room for Jada to enter.

Jada turned to Knox and waved good-bye. And just like that, he drove away.

She gulped down her sadness.

"Who's he?" Sam asked.

"A guy who picked me up last night when my car slid off the road."

"Oh my gosh, Jada. What happened to you last night? You got stitches, you spent the night with some man?"

Jada stepped across the threshold. "It's not what you think. He's…different. Kind, patient, determined. A Christian."

Sam sighed. "They always start off perfect."

Jada rolled her lips between her teeth. "Probably so." She stopped in the living room for a moment to kiss her sleeping nephew on the cheek. He stirred momentarily, then drifted back off to his perfect little world.

With Patrick still in the house, Jada decided it best to go to her room and wait until he left for his shift.

She dropped her bags at the door and shut herself in the sweet silence. Her bones ached now from tiredness. The argument, the crash, walking outside, sleeping in a stranger's bed, saying goodbye to Knox. It was all catching up to her now.

She lay on the bed and closed her eyes.

They always start off perfect.

Jada remembered how happy their mother had been when Sam brought Patrick over for Thanksgiving dinner four years ago. He was a handsome catch— broad chested and ripped with muscles. He had been a perfect gentleman. He'd even said grace before they cut the turkey. Their aunts had congratulated Sam and told her she needed to hold on to him, especially since he was ex-military with benefits.

"He'll be a good provider," their mother had said to Sam after Patrick excused himself to the bathroom. "Paying bills is the most important thing in a marriage."

Jada wondered, even then, how her mother would know what was most important since she'd never been married. She'd never even been in a functional relationship, in Jada's opinion. Yet, somehow, it appeared that Sam was about to beat the odds. She was in love with someone who appeared to be a great guy.

Jada knew better now.

What if Knox is the same? She would much rather be single and rooted in reality than marry a fantasy that turned into a nightmare. *You can't trust people these days.*

But even as she thought those damning words about Knox, a tear rolled from the corner of her eye.

It was nice to imagine.

Jada must have drifted off because half an hour later, she jumped from the bed at the shrilling sounds of Sam and Patrick arguing again. She couldn't put on her headphones, though, because she had to listen to make sure things didn't get physical again.

This is crazy.

Jada checked the time on her phone—10:45.

Thankfully, Patrick needed to leave in the next five minutes or he'd be late for work. Jada waited this one out with a watchful ear.

When he left, she crept out of her room like a soldier coming out of a foxhole. She found Sam sitting at the dining room table, sobbing. "Sam?"

Sam didn't even try to hide the tears. "What?"

Jada rushed to the table and pulled up a chair beside her sister. "Oh, Sam. I'm so sorry you're in this mess."

"That makes two of us."

"What are you going to do? I mean, you can't go on like this forever."

Sam wiped her face. "I don't know. I don't have a job. A place to go."

Jada laughed. "That makes two of us. I've been thinking about moving back with Momma. We could go back together. Start over, just like the day after graduating from high school."

"I don't want to be eighteen again," Sam said. "I couldn't be if I wanted to. I have a child now. He deserves his own room. A backyard. A father. A nice house." She waved her arm around the nicely decorated kitchen. "Momma can't give us anything in that one-bedroom apartment except a couch."

Jada added, "And love. And safety. And a sense of self-worth."

Sam rubbed her forehead. "Don't go there, Jada. I *have* my self-worth."

"No, you don't. Not if you think your face is a punching bag for your own husband."

"He has *never* actually hit me," Sam stated. "Bad words, yes. A restraining move, yes. But Patrick *does not* hit me. He knows the law and he knows I'm not a liar. So when I try to explain what he's doing to file a report, it gets thrown out."

This explanation made no sense. "What if you walked in and saw the daycare worker restraining your child the way Patrick *restrains* you? Or cussing him out the way Patrick cusses at you? Would that be okay with you?"

She shook her head.

"You know, what he does to you is almost worse than hitting. I mean, at least if he hit you, you'd know exactly what happened. But these restraining moves...mashing your face into the floor...it's like, he's playing sadistic mind games. Trying to break you."

Sam sobbed again. "But Patrick used to respect me. He used to treat me like a queen. I don't understand what happened to him."

Jada sat in disbelief, wondering why in the world her sister was crying over this man. Maybe it was beyond her understanding, as Sam had suggested after the fight. Maybe since Jada had never been that strung out over anyone, she couldn't fathom what it was like to be so in love with the memory of who that person used to be that she couldn't see who he was now.

Quite frankly, Jada hoped she'd never be "in love" to such a blinding degree—*if* that was the true definition of love, which she doubted sincerely.

"Look, Sam, I don't know what went wrong or

when, but obviously somewhere the two of you got off track. Do you think maybe you guys can fix it?"

"I already asked him to go to counseling and anger management. He says he doesn't want anybody in our business. He won't go to either one."

Jada closed her eyes as she processed this new information. *What does he mean he won't go?* She fought the urge to tell her sister it was past time to pack up and catch the next bus back to Memphis. Somehow, deep within, Jada didn't feel it was her place to tell a woman to get a divorce. Only Sam could make that decision for herself.

Once, when their mother was dating the postman, Jada had seen him snuggled up at the club with another woman. When she told her mother about what she'd seen, her mother had accused Jada of "keeping up drama." She broke up with the guy for a while, but they eventually got back together, which put a strain on Jada's relationship with her mom. It wasn't until her mother got tired of being played and came to the end of her own rope that she finally broke it off with the guy for good. She did apologize to Jada for being too far gone to listen to reason, and Jada accepted her apology. But the situation taught Jada a lesson. *People believe what they want to believe, especially when romance is involved.* There was no need in trying to run interference for somebody who didn't want a relationship "interfered" with, no matter how dysfunctional it is.

Jada placed a hand on her sister's shoulder. "Sam.

This is *your* life." In the middle of her big speech, Jada forgot what she was going to say. Or maybe she never knew what to say at all. What *could* she say to someone set on living in misery for the sake of her child? Was Sam wrong to make such a sacrifice? Was it so much different than single moms who torture themselves, working three hard minimum-wage jobs and putting up with abusive bosses so their kids can have a roof over their heads?

"And?" Sam interrupted Jada's thoughts.

Jada racked her brain for the right words to complete the lecture. Suddenly, she saw the face of one of Sam's previous boyfriends in her mind, a guy named Mike. Mike had been a drug dealer with an explosive temper. He'd slapped Sam around a few times. Even threatened her life. Now that Jada was thinking about it, Sam's boyfriends were always a little…different. What good would it do if Sam moved back home only to enter another abusive relationship—this time with a kid in tow?

In that short moment of revelation, Jada realized that her sister's problem was bigger than Patrick. The only words Jada could offer were the ones Knox had spoken. "I'm going to pray about this situation."

"I've already begged God to change Patrick."

"Maybe Patrick's not the one who needs the most changing."

Sam's face crinkled. "What are you saying?"

"Hear me out. I'm saying you've been in a string of abusive relationships."

"I know. Pretty unlucky."

"It's not a matter of luck, Sam. I can't put my finger on why you end up with these guys. I only know that my prayer starts with *you*."

Sam rolled her neck to the side. "You need to pray for *yourself* while you're at it. You're the one without a job, without a place to stay. If you ask me, right now we're both in the same boat. Stuck in dead-end situations without a way out except back to our tiny little square ones in Memphis."

Unwilling to argue with her sister, Jada nodded. "Then I guess I'll be praying for both of us."

Chapter 7

Knox raised his hands as his youngest brother, West, led the congregation in praise. With their father out of town celebrating his thirty-fifth anniversary, church attendance was a little lower. People wanted to hear Pastor Reth Stoneworth preach, and for good reason. His father could whoop and holler with the best of them, but only after he thoroughly brought knowledge of God from the Bible.

This Sunday brought Rev. Eli Whittaker to the pulpit to give the sermon. He wasn't much older than Knox. And Knox was only a year older than his bother, Braxton, whom everyone had pegged as the next pastor of their father's church, New Zion.

Knox glanced down the row at Braxton and his fiancé, Tiffany. He wondered if Braxton was ever going to get comfortable in his role as a man of God. And would Tiffany be able to handle the pressure of being the first lady of a mid-sized church? She was teaching now at a charter school, but would she be able to teach and lead the women of New Zion through the next several decades?

After watching his own mother struggle with the role, Knox could only pray for Tiffany. Women in the church could be downright nasty. And it didn't help when some of them wanted to take his mom's place.

He laughed, thinking that if Jada were ever a pastor's wife, she'd put her "hoodness" to good use.

Rainey poked Knox's side. She whispered, "What's

so funny?"

"I was just thinking about something."

"Or *someone*?" Rainey hinted.

Knox gave his sister the slant-eye. "Who are you—the next prophet in the family?"

She elbowed him harder.

"Stop being so violent."

They both laughed as Rev. Whittaker called the building to prayer in preparation for his sermon. When he instructed the congregation to turn to Isaiah 43, Knox spread open his Bible while Rainey scrolled through her cell phone.

He teased her by shaking his head.

"What? There's nothing wrong with looking at the scriptures on your phone."

Knox said, "Not the same as having it right here in your hand." He patted his tried and true leather-bound sword.

Rainey pointed at herself. "Truth be told, you're supposed to hide the word in your *heart*."

She had him on that point. "What are we going to do with you?"

Rainey laughed and Knox had to join her. His little sister was becoming quite the young lady.

Rev. Whittaker spend the first fifteen minutes of his sermon giving them the context, then he read verses 1-7. Knox reread verse seven as the Holy Spirit seemed to pull him aside for a mini-sermon. *Even every one that is called by my name: for I have created him for my glory, I have formed him; yea, I have made him.*

Everyone was made for God's glory. *Everyone?* Somehow this was sinking into Knox's heart real deep for the first time. He knew he had already been reconciled to God through Christ—but the idea that *everyone* else was on earth to glorify God? *Including Jada? Including Dominique?*

Everyone sure wasn't acting like they belonged to God. *Everyone doesn't agree.*

Knox rejoined the main sermon, giving Rev. Whittaker his attention. "My brothers and sisters in the Lord, the problem is that we live in a very deceptive world, particularly in this country. We are bombarded with false philosophies and made-up truths that have no foundation in the Word. We've confused the American dream with God's dream and we're preaching that God also wants everyone to own a piece of land, build a house on it, throw up a white picket fence around it, and put two-point-five children and a dog in it."

"Dogs belong in the back yard," Knox heard one of the older ladies behind him ad-lib.

"The problem is," Rev. Whittaker continued, "what if the American Dream and God's Dream aren't the same for you. What if God would rather you, your spouse, and your seven kids live in a remote village caring for orphans?"

"Seven kids?" Rainey and half the church balked.

"Uh huh," the preacher continued, "what if what God wants for you has nothing to do with things and everything to do with Him? These verses tell us that He gathers, He reconciles, He created His people for *Him*.

Not us. *Him*."

Knox felt an "ouch" coming, though he wasn't sure exactly where he'd been hit.

"Let's take for example romance."

"Uh oh," somebody exclaimed, which caused a round of laughter in the building.

"Speak on it!" someone else yelled.

"Thank you. I do believe I will," Rev. Whittaker joked. "You ever heard of the term soul mates?"

The church affirmed him.

"Let me explain. A soul mate, by most definitions, is someone who *gets* you. They understand you without verbal communication. You can finish each other's sentences because you think alike. The two of you possess an inexplicable chemistry—you just clicked when you first met. In short, you were created for one another—destined for one another. You feel me?"

Everyone agreed.

Knox listened with both natural and spiritual ears now. He had spoken to the Lord about Jada after he dropped her off. Anything said about relationships between a man and a woman would definitely be logged in his system right about now.

"Well, let me tell you a little something about soul mates. Y'all ready?"

"Yeah!" the people roared.

"Soul mates is nowhere in the Bible."

Rainey gasped. "Say it ain't so."

Knox glanced down at her shocked face.

"There is one reference to 'the one' in Song of

Solomon chapter three, which is largely a picture of God's love for us. But this notion of a 'soul mate' does not have its roots in the Word. The history of this term goes back to Greek mythology. In a book entitled *The Symposium* by Plato, he records the dialogue of several men at a party, as told to him by someone else. So first of all, Plato wasn't even *at* the party.

"Anyway, Plato writes that these guys, including his mentor Socrates, got tired of hearing the woman at the party playing her flute. So one of them decided— hey! Let's everybody give some speeches about love! So after a while, this guy named Aristophanes—who had been drinking at this party for two days straight— spouted off his theory. He said that a long time ago, people had four legs, four arms, and two heads. They were shaped like balls. They kind of walked-ran, twice the speed that you and I can walk. I don't even know what that looks like, but I can tell you right now we're already a long way from Genesis."

"Huh?" Knox huffed.

"So one day," Rev. Whittaker said, "the two-headed creatures got an idea. They would find a way to ascend to the gods. Of course, Zeus didn't like that idea. They thought about killing the people, but then there would be no one to make sacrifices. So Zeus came up with a plan to split them in two and give everyone two arms, only two legs, and one head. With the help of Apollo, the people were restructured and reordered into separate beings. According to this theory, people will never be satisfied in life until they find their soul mate, their other half. The person they used to be connected to but Zeus split them apart. That, my friends, is where we got the notion of soul mates."

"Wow."

Rainey took the word right out of Knox's mouth.

Rev. Whittaker cleared his throat. "Now. Fast-forward twenty-five hundred years or so, here we are today. We've got people—Christian people, too!—getting married because they believe they've found their soul mates. And we've got people getting divorce because the person they *thought* was their soul mate turned out to be...not. And we're making covenant decisions based on the second-hand account of a philosophy spoken by a drunk man at a party!"

The saints grumbled and oooh-ed at this news.

"Saints of God, this is what the Bible calls 'deceptive philosophies' in Colossians two and eight; cooky man-made concepts that we've failed to cross-check with the Word of God!"

Rainey whispered to Knox, "Did you know this?"

"No."

"Oh my God—and I don't mean that like in vain! I can't believe we all bought into this," she shrieked, which blended in with the sound of scales falling off eyes and crashing to the floor for all the other believers in the church that morning.

"Now, let me bring this on back to Isaiah chapter forty-three. You see, no one was made for *you*. No one was made for *me*. We were all made to glorify Him. If the soul mate theory were true, that would mean unmarried Christians could never be complete, and that can't be true because Jesus wasn't married and Paul didn't recommend marriage for everyone. *Christ* is our completer. When two people who are complete in Christ get married, the purpose is two-fold—to paint a picture of Christ's love for the church, and to accomplish a God-given task that turns around and honors Him some mo'!"

The members and guests were getting riled up now, standing to their feet and waving at Rev. Whittaker.

Meanwhile, Knox was still back at the party with Plato's drunk friends. Having taken a few electives in psychology, Knox was familiar with the noted Greek philosophers, who were known for their wine, their long speeches, and polytheism. Knox was also familiar with the Socratic method of questioning, which always leads a person back to themselves as the ultimate source of knowledge and truth. It made perfect sense that those men would sit around giving speeches to one another as a form of entertainment. What *didn't* make sense was how this "soul mate" theory had lasted for centuries and even been adopted by Bible-believing Christians without any investigation whatsoever—himself included.

When compared with the light of the Word, the soul mate theory couldn't be true.

It would take Knox a minute to digest the sermon. He had to re-think his marriage game now. He'd wanted someone to be *his* wife. He wanted to be the object of her affection and vice versa. And it wouldn't hurt if she was a beauty to behold.

But now, thanks to Isaiah 43, Knox felt led to submit his mind to renewal. His marriage would have a mission even greater than experiencing the favor of God and raising great kids. If and when he got married, it would be for and to God's glory, the same way it had been for his great-great grandfather, Isaac Stoneworth, when he and his wife, Evelina, became a pillar of strength in their community after Emancipation.

How or if that sermon was an answer to his prayer about Jada was yet to be seen.

Chapter 8

One good thing about working for a major chain of pet clinics was the fact that Mayfield specialized in household pets. Time in veterinary school had prepared Knox for operating on animals from turtles to horses, but the contract at Mayfield meant he didn't have to remember everything at once.

This morning had been routine—spays and neuters followed by check-us, vaccinations, and other appointments. The newest vets handled the walk-ins. Knox had been at Mayfield for two years. He was no longer the rookie now that they'd hired Dr. Fritz Lewis six months ago. Knox had to admit, though, that he missed working with the walk-ins. Many were people who didn't routinely take their animals to see vets; they only brought them in when there was a problem. The problem was often pretty far gone, which presented special challenges. That's what Knox missed—the challenges.

Every once in a while, the routine surgeries posed threw a curve ball. Knox was often amazed at how God not only gave every human being a unique thumbprint, but He also made each animal all its own as well; no two exactly alike.

Surgery time provided an opportunity for Knox to meditate not only on the marvel of God's creation, but on the issues in his life. The operating room was quiet. The animal was asleep. His assistant was monitoring vital signs and Knox preferred to keep conversation to a minimum. Before coming to work, Knox had spent half an hour or so in prayer and reading scriptures for wisdom and guidance about Jada. *Is she safe at her sister's house? Is she someone I can trust? Do I reach out to her again? If so, how?* He had not exchanged numbers with her. The only way he knew to get in contact with her was to return to her sister's house.

Knox finally got an opportunity to take a breather when the office closed for lunch. He scrubbed his hands clean and rested for a minute in the breakroom. He took a moment to text his friend, Allen, about Jada's car: *A—don't fix it. She said let it go. What I owe you?*

Knox bought a pack of peanuts from the vending machine and drank one of the bottled waters available to all employees in the refrigerator.

"How's it going?" Dr. Lewis asked as he sat for a moment as his food warmed in the microwave.

"Pretty good. How are you?"

"Tired. Long weekend."

"Same here," Knox agreed.

Fritz smirked. "Hot date?"

"No. She was nice-looking, but I wouldn't call it a date."

Fritz smacked Knox on the back. "Oh! A one-nighter! I didn't think you had it in you."

The microwave beeped. Fritz got his food and rejoined Knox at the table.

Knox shook his head. "Naaaa. I'm not the one." This conversation was beginning to annoy Knox.

Dr. Fritz Lewis was in his mid-twenties. Blondehair and blue eyes. Worked out. The kind of guy Knox imagined the ladies swooned over in the club, especially when he mentioned that he was a doctor, which was probably the first sentence out of his mouth.

"Should have known. Church boy," Fritz teased.

"Through and through. You should come with me—first Saturdays we have a men's fellowship. Inspiration, motivation. Networking."

"Networking?"

"Yeah." Knox knew that the prospect of personal advancement would catch Fritz's attention. But if Fritz heard the life-changing gospel of Jesus Christ, he just might leave the fellowship with more than he'd bargained for.

"I'll think about it." Fritz leaned in. "Mayfield might be merging with Cox & Leimberg soon."

"Where'd you hear that?"

"Buried in a report online. A rumor, for now."

"Mmm." Knox wasn't alarmed. A merger would only mean more customers, greater job stability.

"Mergers are murder. New guys coming in, pushing the old guys out. Changing the system. Rocking the boat. We'll have to fight to keep our jobs."

Knox noted the glint of fear in Fritz's eyes. He felt sorry for people like Fritz who didn't have the assurance of a God whose plans for them were good, who worked all things for their good. If only Fritz knew.

As Fritz went on and on about how terrible things could get for their company and for the world in general, Knox felt the Holy Spirit pricking him inside. He prayed silently, asking the Lord for the right words to minister to his younger co-worker. He doubted there would be a full-blown conversion in the breakroom, but he didn't want to miss this opportunity to plant a seed or water a seed that, perhaps, another believer had planted previously.

When there was a break in Fritz's monologue, Knox said, "You're right, bro. This world is crazy. We can't control the circumstances. That's why we need an inner peace, you know?"

Fritz exhaled. Then he chuckled at Knox. "You're not the typical preacher's kid. They were always the ones sneaking girls and weed into the woods at summer church camps."

Knox laughed. "Can't say I wasn't *tempted* to do those things—I'm not perfect. I've been blessed to see, at an early age, that the right way is usually the path that'll end up costing you less, with a better outcome in the end. Why complicate life, you know what I'm sayin'?"

His co-worker's eyes were fixed on his bowl of spaghetti, but Knox knew that Fritz was listening. He added, "The truth will set you free, doc."

Fritz chewed. "That's what they say." He held up his water bottle for a toast with Knox. "Amen."

Knox followed suit, tapping the side of his bottle against Fritz's. "Amen."

"Hey—you think the Cowboys have a chance this year?" Fritz asked.

Knox allowed the flow of the conversation to change courses. He was confident that his watering had been successful and entrusted the real growth to God.

"Only if the key players stay healthy," Knox said.

The two men enjoyed a spirited debate about which was the best team in the NFC East, followed by good-humored political banter.

Knox's phone buzzed with a text from Allen: OK. You want to come get the stuff from her car? He smiled to himself as he typed: Yes. I'll be there around 4.

He could hardly wait for his last scheduled appointment at 3:30. Joo-joo, a temperamental tabby, had gotten into a fight with a neighbor's cat a week earlier, and a tiny bite-wound had gotten infected. Knox quickly cleaned and covered the wound. He wrote a prescription for an antibiotic.

Joo-joo's happy owner whisked the cat away, and Knox whisked himself over to Allen's garage.

The shed smelled of oil and metal. Sixties R&B crackled from an old radio sitting atop a case of tools. Two men were working under cars, while a third man was behind the hood of another. Knox greeted them and walked on to the office, where he knew he'd find Allen.

His shirt was stained black in two spots, despite the fact that Allen had recently decided to leave the hard work to his employees. Allen had been working on cars since he and Knox were eleven years old. His repair and maintenance shop was the only one Knox trusted with his own vehicles.

"'Sup?" Knox gave Allen the bro-shake.

"It's all on you," Allen said jovially. He sat behind his desk again. "Man, that car was in terrible shape. It's a miracle it was still running. I've never seen so much duct tape holding a vehicle together."

"She did say she was broke," Knox said.

"She wasn't lying," Allen attested. "Here." He gave Knox a large manila envelope. "She had a lot of papers in the trunk. Looked important. Thought she might want them back."

Knox grasped the package. "Thanks."

"Does she have the title?"

"I don't know. Would it help if she signed it over?"

"Yeah. Otherwise, I'll have to file a mechanic's lien and send her notices before I can scrap it, legally."

"Got it. I'll get the title from her." Knox could have done a cartwheel. Now he had a valid reason to contact Jada again.

"Great. Saves me trouble. Whose car is it, anyway? Rainey's?"

"No. She's a woman I met recently."

Allen crossed his arms and tilted back in his chair. "You're finally getting over Dominique, huh?"

"Man, I *been* past that chick," Knox defended himself.

"Good thing." Allen straightened his chair. "She brings her car in here sometimes. Wearing tight dresses. Flirting with my employees. Trying to keep tabs on you."

"On me?"

"Yeah. I had another black Jeep with tan, leather

interior in here the last time she brought in her car for an oil change. She runs into my office, asking me if it's yours. I told her I didn't know whose it was. I wasn't here when the owner dropped it off. So she asks me to look up the bill and I told her to get out. So then she waits across the street. For three hours! To see if it was you."

Knox muttered, "Wow." Dominique must really be having some trouble in her marriage.

"Anyway, I'm glad she's out of your life," Allen said. "Keep movin' until you find the right one."

"Word," Knox said. "You sure I don't owe you anything?"

"We're straight. If I get the title. I'm sure I can break even."

Knox gave Allen some dap. "Thanks, man. I'll talk to you later."

Back in his car, Knox tore through the envelope's seal and searched for something bearing Jada's contact information. He found the treasure easily. Front and center on her resume were her current mailing address, phone number, and email address.

Knox snooped a bit more.

Jada Moniece Jones. Graduate of Southwest Tennessee Community College– Accounting. She'd finished high school a few years after him, which he figured meant she was around twenty-eight. She had a solid work history since earning her associate's degree with a strong GPA.

She's smart. Somehow, that made him happy. If she

could do well at a smaller college, she had what it took to earn a 4-year degree. A master's. A doctorate. He wondered why she hadn't pursued further education. He thought of his sister, Rainey, and how she'd made the choice to go all-in with her degrees. He wanted that for Jada, a sense of accomplishment that could never be taken away.

He called the number listed on the resume and sighed with relief when her familiar voice answered, "Hello?"

"Hello, Jada. This is Knox Stoneworth. How are you?"

"I'm…I'm fine. How are you?"

He could hear the shock and the smile in her voice. "Listen, my friend who towed your car said you'd left some important paperwork in your car. I hope you don't mind that I got your number from your belongings."

"No, no problem at all. I'm glad you called."

"Me, too," Knox said.

The sweet silence between them confirmed his hope that Jada also wanted to keep in touch.

Knox said, "My friend who towed your car is more than happy to get rid of it. But he needs the title to make things easier."

"No problem. I have it here. You're welcome to come by."

"Perfect. How about an hour from now?"

"I look forward to it, Knox."

"Same here."

Chapter 9

Jada's chest bubbled with excitement. She was seeing Knox Stoneworth again in ten minutes. "How do I look?" she asked Sam.

Sam stood behind Jada and glanced in the full-length mirror on the back of Jada's closet. Together, they surveyed Jada's ensemble—stone-washed blue jeans, a bulky pink and black long-sleeved, crew-necked Nike shirt, and a pair of pink Crocks.

"This is not a particularly attractive outfit," Sam noted as she propped the baby up on her hip.

"I know, but it's all I have outside of professional clothes. It's not like I've been all up in the club."

"You gotta at least put on a necklace. And these earrings are microscopic, like you're a kindergartner who just got her ears pierced."

Jada laughed with her sister.

"I'm going to get you a different shirt."

Sam left the room. Jada removed the shirt she was wearing and waited for her sister's return. The house was silent. This was one of the better days in her sister's household. Mondays and Tuesdays were Patrick's off days. He usually slept late, which meant a morning of peace and quiet. Then he'd get up and eat whatever Jada prepared and lock himself in his man-cave. There were no arguments. No put-downs.

Come to think of it, Patrick hadn't even made any snide comments about the baked chicken or the mashed potatoes Jada cooked. Maybe the Lord was involving

Himself already.

Sam returned with a gray V-cut shirt and a white tank to go underneath. "This will at least hint at your curves."

"I don't want him to be turned on by my curves," Jada fussed. "For once, I want a man to like me for *me*." She pulled the tight shirt over her head nonetheless.

"But your curves are a part of you." Sam poked out her lips. "I know if I had a body like yours, you couldn't tell me nothin'.

"And it wouldn't hurt if you tightened up that interview suit of yours. People like attractiveness in an employee."

"You've gone too far now, Sam. I worked hard to earn my degree. My future employer needs to look at my resume, not my behind."

"Suit yourself."

Sam gave Jada a pair of blinged-out, loopy earrings and a silver necklace with a heart-shaped pendant. She pushed a swath of lipstick onto Jada's lips. She swiveled Jada toward the mirror again. "Much better. Despite the big band-aid on your head."

Now that she was a little more snazzy, Jada was ready to see Knox again. She kissed the baby for good measure. His sweet cheeks and lotion-scent made Jada feel alive all the more.

The doorbell rang. "That's him!" Jada announced unnecessarily. She was more nervous than she should be. More nervous than she had ever been about seeing a guy.

"I'll let him in. You stay here so you can make an entrance," Sam ordered.

"What? That's crazy. This is not prom night," Jada quipped.

"Look. You want to 'wow' him or what?"

"I want to 'hello' him, not make him drool."

"Like I said, your body is a wow-factor in and of itself. You need to dress it up. Make it pop. The way to a man's heart is through his eyes, little sister. Once you've got his attention, your conversation, your personality takes it from there."

"If you say so," Jada agreed as Sam left the room.

As Jada waited for her sister's cue, she wondered if she should be taking relationship advice from Sam. If this was the norm—capturing a man's attention with your body first, making a grand entrance for a small meeting—what other games were women playing in order to catch a man who turned out to be not even worth the bait?

Jada snatched off the tight shirt and put back on her oversized top. She didn't want to be anything but herself when she saw Knox again. He had seen her at her worst and still liked what he saw. Jada saw no need to show him what he wasn't going to get on a regular basis…if they had a future together.

Jada walked out of her bedroom and interrupted Sam's light, stalling conversation with Knox in the foyer.

Sam's eyes questioned Jada as she took in the

reversal of appearance.

Jada ignored her sister and focused on Knox, who was beautiful enough for three or four people put together. "Hi!"

Knox's face brightened. "Hello. You look great."

Jada smirked at Sam. "Thank you."

"It's the earrings," Sam said.

Jada slapped her sister's arm. "Anyway."

She and Knox shared a loose hug. Even with an appropriate space between them, she could feel the raised muscles in his arms and chest. She thanked God for making men so very different from women and also prayed that she wouldn't become so engrossed in his looks that she lost all sense.

"Here are your personal items." He gave her the large envelope.

"Thank you." Jada set them on a half-table against the wall.

Sunlight streamed through the front door's stained glass, beckoning Jada toward fresh air. "You want to walk to the park?"

"Sure," Knox said.

She turned to her sister again. "See ya later."

"You two behave yourselves," Sam chided.

"Yes, ma'am," Knox played along.

Once outside the house, they strolled down the sidewalk, with Jada leading the way up the street and toward the community playground.

"How was church yesterday?" she asked him.

"Amazing. My father is the pastor but my parents

are out of town, so we had a guest preacher. He blew our minds by comparing common beliefs with Greek myths. Sent me to my knees for sure."

"Sounds interesting," Jada said. "Any scriptures you can share?"

"Definitely. I can text them to you."

"I'd appreciate it. Thank you."

Two little girls on bicycles breezed past, taunting each other in high shrills. "You can't beat me!"

"Yes, I can!" The younger one pedaled faster, trying to catch up.

Knox laughed. "Those were the days, huh? Racing down the street on bicycles, not a care in the world."

Jada shook her head. "Ummm...no. I don't have those memories, either." Once again, the fact that they had grown up in two different worlds reared its ugly head.

"You never rode a bicycle?"

"No. My mom didn't get us bikes."

"Oh."

Jada was glad he didn't say anything insensitive. For his politeness, she'd give him the hood explanation. "She had her reasons. First of all, we lived on the third floor of an apartment complex. Lugging those bikes up and down stairs would have been a pain, and there's no such thing as leaving your toys outside in the hood. Secondly, there were too many crazy dogs in the neighborhood. A pit bull on a chain will just about break its neck to chase a kid who seems like she's running. Third, we didn't know our neighbors like that.

People move in and out of low-income areas. She didn't feel safe letting me and my sister roam the streets on our bicycles with people she didn't know. So, no. We didn't have bicycles."

"I'm sorry to hear that," Knox said, looking down at his feet. "What did you do for fun?"

"Watch TV. Read. We used to play video games until someone broke into our apartment and stole our entertainment system."

"Really?"

"Yep." She shrugged. "That's the breaks sometimes."

"Man. That's terrible."

"You never had anything stolen from you?"

"Not that I can remember."

"Must be nice."

They rounded the corner of the block. The park was in view. A mother with two pre-school age boys was pushing her children in the swings.

Jada guessed that Knox had memories like these, too. With his father playing professional football, his mother probably hadn't worked. He might have even had a nanny.

The swing set in her neighborhood never seemed to be able to keep its chains. People cut them and used them for other purposes like tying up those pit bulls, creating car-towing devices, or whatever else they could rig with the sturdy, heavy-weight material. Nothing that could be detached, repurposed, and/or resold had a chance at their playground.

"I'll race you to the slide," Knox challenged.

"No. We are too old for a race," Jada said. Then she pointed down at the sidewalk. "What's that?"

When Knox looked down, Jada took off running, giving herself enough of a head start to beat him. She sprinted the fifteen yards to the base of the slide and tagged it. "Beatcha!"

"That's because you cheated!" Knox objected with a hearty smile. "Plus I'm wearing professional shoes. You wait until I get my kicks on."

"I ran track in high school. Shoes might not help you much," Jada bragged.

"We'll see."

Jada climbed the ladder and took a victory trip down the spiraled slide. "This is a nice park. All parts in place."

Knox met her at the landing. "Not like the hood, I'm guessing?"

"Naaa. We had those metal slides. Mostly too hot or too cold outside to really enjoy them."

The mother who had been pushing her kids on the slide was walking away with them now, one holding each hand.

"Guess we can have the swings now." Jada chuckled to herself.

"Works for me."

Jada sat in the hard, green seat, pushing off slightly.

Knox sat but there was no room for his legs to fold. He could only rock slightly.

But at least she and Knox would have something in

common—being African-American in a white-dominated world. Jada commented, "Some things doesn't change, no matter where you go."

"What?" Knox asked.

"White people. Scared of black people."

"Maybe they've been here for a while. Maybe it's time for the kids to go home and take baths and eat dinner."

Jada narrowed her eyes as she looked over. "The moment we got here?"

"Stranger things have happened."

Jada threw her head back and swung higher. "Why are you such an idealist?"

"Why are you such a pessimist?" he countered. "I don't waste my time conjuring up negative motives for total strangers. Even if people's actions do seem odd, I give them the benefit of the doubt. Saves me from a lot of stress. Frees my mind to focus on things that actually benefit me."

This man is impossible. Jada opened her mouth to explain the entire world to him, but didn't know where to start. She truly felt sorry for him because, one day, he would see things as they were, not through the buffer of all his father's money, his education, and his cushy upbringing. People like him ended up going crazy when they came up against a brick wall in their lives. Unlike her, they didn't know how to overcome the impossible.

"Knox. In case you haven't noticed, it's a dog-eat-dog world. You have to look out for yourself because no one else will. My mother taught me that I have two strikes against me—I'm a woman and I'm black. You might have triple-strikes against you because you're a black man. You feel me?"

"No," Knox said. "Because my father taught me that if God is for me, He's more than the whole world against me. So I don't build my life around who may or may not like me. It's irrelevant. I wouldn't be where I am today if I'd walked into my vet-school classes worried about who was trying to stab me in the back. Couldn't waste my energy on that. I don't think you should, either. Especially not if it detracts from the simple joys in life, like going to a park."

Jada posed, "So if a police officer pulls you over in your nice, shiny SUV for no reason, you won't be upset?"

"That particular situation is not an *if*, it's a *when*," Knox said.

Finally, we agree on something.

"I'm not happy about it. I file a complaint, follow up with his supervisor. Long-term, I research my local candidates and vote accordingly, support organizations that have my best interest at heart. But in the moment that I'm parked on the road's shoulder, no. I'm not afraid because no weapon formed against me prospers."

Knox's words and the conviction in his stern expression were enough to make Jada take off swinging a little higher. She knew from lessons she'd attended at her grandmother's church that Knox was quoting scriptures from the Bible. This idea of his, that what he'd learned in the Bible actually applied to his *real* life, was...*new*.

Everything about Christian life was new, really, but what if? What if Christ died and left her the kind of life where she didn't have to worry? Where what He said in His word trumped the world?

This was too much to handle for now. Jada slowed her pace on the swing and wiggled her way around to another topic. "How was work today?"

"Good. A few surgeries. Appointments. No euthanasia candidates. No trauma—at least not any for me. How was your day?"

"It started off well. Had an interview, but I knew after the first few minutes that I wasn't going to get the job."

"And you knew that because..." Knox led.

"Because of this bandage on my head. Looks like I've been in a street fight. The interviewer spent more minutes looking at my forehead than my eyes. So insensitive. What if I'd had some kind of birthmark there? Would she have stared at it the whole time, too?"

"Possibly," Knox agreed. "You got any more interviews scheduled?"

"No. Still filling out applications online. If I don't find anything this week, I'm moving back to Memphis."

Knox reached her swing's chains and slowed her to a halt. "Wait...moving back to Memphis?"

"Yeah. I can't stay here forever and mooch off my sister and my brother-in-law. Besides, I feel like Patrick and I are one centimeter from having an Ike-and-Tina-Turner moment."

Knox's brows furrowed. "If he hits you, Jada...we're going to have a serious problem."

She liked how he said *we*. "You've been worrying about me since the moment we met. Please stop."

Knox nodded. "It's my pleasure to care for a damsel in distress."

"I am far from the princess trapped at the top of a castle. I prefer to rescue myself."

"Impossible," Knox disagreed. "If you could rescue yourself, you never would have gotten trapped in the first place. Such is the story of mankind."

Jada's swing stilled completely in Knox's grasp. The heat of his gaze filled her heart.

"So may I help you try to find a job? I've got friends. Connections in the city."

Jada peered at him. "Why are you so nice to me?"

"Why not?"

"What's your motive?" she rephrased the question.

"To be honest, I wasn't sure at first. But now, I'm thinking it's to show you that someone can be nice without a self-serving motive. Even if you have to move back to Memphis, at least you'll go knowing that not everyone is dead-set on hurting you."

The very possibility that there was such goodness to be found in people made Jada think of how different her mind had been when she'd gone to church with her co-worker. The preacher had talked about Jesus as though His whole purpose was to see people free. And she had believed on Him, His goodness. She had even started reading the Bible and thinking about life differently, until she'd run into that problem at her previous job, her evil boss, and life with Sam and the brother-in-law who was actually a wolf in sheep's clothing. Those things—life—had stolen the new hope she'd found in Christ.

But now, He seemed to be restoring it through Knox.

"I appreciate your kindness," Jada said with genuine gratitude.

"You're welcome."

Knox walked her back to Sam's house. He waited inside for Jada to give him the signed car title.

"Good riddance," she said as she handed him the papers.

"Better things coming, right?" he suggested.

"If you say so."

"I always speak what I want to occur in my life."

"Fine," Jada relented, "I'll say it. One day, I'm going to have a better car than the one I'm losing now."

"That's what I'm talkin' about." Knox winked. "But first, you need a job. With your permission, I'll share your resume. I kept the one I used to retrieve your contact information."

"No problem. I'll follow up on the resumes I've already submitted."

"Touch bases tomorrow?" he proposed.

"Yeah."

And then he did something Jada wasn't ready for.

He kissed her on the cheek. "Have a good night."

"You, too." She could barely speak.

Lord, please don't make me move back to Memphis.

Chapter 10

"Hey, Braxton," Knox said. "Since you got that big school contract with Dad's friend, you need some help? I know someone with accounting experience. She can help you count all the dough."

To himself, Knox sounded like a telemarketer. Pathetic. But if it meant Jada didn't have to return to Memphis, he was willing to humiliate himself.

"Man, I wish you had called last month. I just hired someone to do my books. Sorry. You tried Paige? She might have something open in her division."

Knox spent his entire lunch break calling friends and family who might be able to help Jada. With her following up and him putting out feelers, they should be able to come up with something soon.

Lord, please don't let her move back to Memphis any time soon.

He finished his workday at the office, then checked his phone again as he walked to his car. Paige had texted him about a possible position at her retail company, and his other cousin, Shiloh, pointed Knox to a link for an accounting opening for his employer.

He called Jada to share the prospects. When she answered the phone, he immediately heard yelling in the background. "Jada?"

"Yeah," she said.

"Umm...is now a good time?"

"No. As you can hear, my sister and her husband are having a disagreement."

The words he heard signaled more than a disagreement. They were goin' at it ferociously.

"Shall I call you later, or do you need me to come get you?"

"No. I'm fine. Just text me what you'd like to say. I gotta go. Bye." She ended the call.

Just listening to the chaos second-hand had jarred Knox. He couldn't imagine what it was like to live in that environment day in and day out. What was worse, a baby lived there, too.

Knox set his phone on the passenger's seat of his car and prayed. "Lord, You know what's happening in that household. You know the frustrations and issues Jada's sister and brother-in-law are dealing with. I pray that You would show Yourself to them—together or separately, however You wish to do it. Bring peace for Your sake, Jada's sake, and the child's sake. And protect Jada's mind and heart until You open another door for her. Be glorified as You show them all a different way. Your way. In Jesus' name I pray, Amen."

***

Jada was too angry to be embarrassed when Knox called. Patrick had crossed the line. Some woman had called the house earlier and told Sam to "keep herself up" if she wanted to keep her man. Sam, of course, had interrupted Patrick's "quiet time" in the man-cave.

The argument flowed from the man-cave to the living room, then to the kitchen.

"Who is she?"

"Someone who knows more than you, obviously!" Patrick retorted.

Jada dared not clamp on her headphones again. She needed to listen in case there was need for another intervention.

Jada continued texting Knox, trying to sooth the anxiety that seeped through every word on the screen. She did her best to assure him that she was perfectly fine. They needed to focus on her job hunt, not her brother-in-law.

After several rounds of texts, Knox focused on the topic at hand. They agreed to talk again soon.

As the argument ensued in the kitchen, Patrick said he didn't know who the woman was or how she'd gotten Sam's number, but that whoever she was had been right—Sam did need to step up her appearance if she wanted to prevent him from fooling around.

"Have you lost your mind?" Sam screamed.

Patrick didn't answer.

Sam's voice went missing.

All that could be heard was the tick-tock of the baby's automatic swing chair.

Jada's heart thudded.

She heard glass shatter and knew something was happening. Remembering her last conversation with Sam about Patrick's particular form of abuse and how police disregarded the reports, Jada quickly grabbed her cell phone. She turned on the camera and tucked it into her plaid shirt pocket, lens facing outward.

Accompanied by a digital witness, Jada threw the door of her bedroom open and rushed to help her sister. Though she was approaching from the side, she could clearly see that Patrick had Sam's neck in the crook of his elbow. Sam couldn't breathe.

Jada grabbed a bar stool and slammed it against Patrick's back. He and Sam fell forward onto the kitchen table.

Sam gasped for air.

Patrick groaned, rubbing his side. "You crazy?"

"Takes one to know one," Jada spewed. She was still holding the chair in case he tried to attack.

"You're going down today. Assault."

"I was defending my sister."

"You have no proof."

"That's what you think," Jada said. "I got it all on video." She tapped her pocket.

Sam, who was sitting on the floor, looked up at Jada with an increased fear.

Patrick gritted his teeth and lunged at Jada, slinging the chair out of her grasp. He ripped the phone from her pocket, slammed it on the floor, and reduced it to pieces with three quick stomps.

"Where's your proof now, ma'am?"

Jada bluffed. "I have automatic back-up to the cloud." She pointed at the ceiling.

"It doesn't work that fast," Patrick said.

"You wanna bet?" Jada threatened.

"Out!" he spat. "Out. Now. And don't come back. Ever!" His nose flared as he fumed.

Though she'd played it off well, Jada was still in shock at seeing her phone destroyed. She was so angry, she could cry. She wouldn't give Patrick the satisfaction, however.

Sam stood. Took Jada by the arm. "Let's go."

Jada tried to jerk away, but Sam held on tighter and said into Jada's ear. "You need to be outside. In public view. Now."

Déjà vu. Jada stepped outside the house again. Kicked out for the second time in three days. *No, this is worse than Déjà vu.* She had only a purse because Sam had insisted they get out before Patrick "really blows up."

Sam unlocked her car doors. Jada entered the passenger's side. Sam drove off, then stopped around the corner from her house. She put the car in park. "Jada," she panted, "I've never seen Patrick so angry in all my life."

"I don't care."

"I had to get you out of there. I didn't know what he might do to you," she squeaked as a tear fell down her brown cheek. "I gotta go back, though. I wouldn't dare leave the baby with him for long."

"Right. Don't worry about me. You're the one who's married to him. Living with him. Raising a child with him. What are you going to do? It's only a matter of time before things get worse. You *have* to leave," Jada pleaded with her only sister.

"We're fine. I just have to...try not to make him so mad." She bore the onus for Patrick's actions. "I shouldn't have asked him about the woman."

"You had every right to know about the woman. He had no right to physically attack you."

"It wasn't an attack, Jada. You're exaggerating. And he only did it to calm me down."

Jada felt like slapping her sister silly. *Who in her right mind thinks like this?* Maybe that was the problem. Perhaps Sam wasn't in her right mind. Maybe the abuse had warped her sense of herself and reality as a whole.

Sam sniffed. Dried her face. "You think maybe you can go to Knox's house?"

"No. I don't know where he lives. And I don't have his cell number, thanks to Patrick."

"I'll get you another phone tomorrow. You can come back to the house tomorrow, too. Around eleven, after Patrick leaves for work. But tonight...we need a plan B."

The abrupt switch in Sam's tone from panicked to cool and collected made Jada wonder all the more if her sister was sane. She was talking as though nothing life-threatening or traumatic had just happened. "Sam, we don't even have a Plan A. How are you on to Plan B already? Wake up! Stop acting like everything's okay!"

Sam turned her head from Jada and looked out the window.

Jada realized the last thing her sister needed was someone else yelling at her, but how else could she get it through her sister's head that Patrick was a wife-beater? Even though his fist never made contact with her face, he was abusive. And yet, he'd somehow brainwashed her into believing that he wasn't. Jada had to give him his due. He was a master manipulator.

"There's a really nice shelter about ten minutes from here," Sam offered. "They house women and men, but the men are in a separate part of the building."

"You've been there?"

"Yeah. The first time we had a really bad argument. Patrick pulled his service weapon on me. Scared me half to death." She tried to belittle the incident with a slight smile. "But that only happened once."

"He doesn't *have* to do it again," Jada whispered, nearly in tears. "He *knows* it'll stay in the back of your mind forever."

"Well. Do you want to go to the shelter?"

"Is there another option?"

"You got any other friends? Former co-workers?"

"Every number I had was in my phone."

"I'm sorry."

There truly was no other reasonable option. Jada sighed. "The shelter it is."

Chapter 11

"Dr. Stoneworth?" his assistant called Knox's name.

Knox snapped back to reality. "I'm sorry. What?"

"You want me to ask Mrs. Collins to reschedule for tomorrow, or can you see her dog now?"

Knox checked his watch—*4:58*. He had no recollection of the past ten minutes because he had zoned out, thinking about Jada. Three days had passed since he'd been in contact with Jada. Her phone was going straight to voicemail, and she wasn't responding to texts. If he didn't hear from her in the next couple of days, he would have to make an unannounced visit to her sister's house.

Maybe helping a pet would ease his mind for a bit. "No problem. I'll see her."

"I'll put her in room twelve. Shelly's staying a little later. She can help if needed."

"Fine. Have a good weekend."

"You, too."

He didn't know who Mrs. Collins was or what her pet's issue might be, but it didn't matter.

Knox forced himself to finish up documentation so he could see this dog, complete his workday, and leave. Not that he had anything important to do. Anyone to see. Truth be told, he missed Jada. In less than a week's time, she had claimed a piece of his heart. It felt good to have someone occupying his lonely heart again. If only she would call him back.

Papers aside, Knox looped his stethoscope around his neck and proceeded from his office to room twelve. Accepting after-hours appointments was simply good customer service.

Upon entrance to the room, Knox's torso tightened. *Dominique.*

She wore a casual denim dress with a brown belt cinched around her small waist. The dainty, yet defined curves of her thighs and calves flowed beyond the short hem of the dress.

Her beauty was undeniable.

"Hi, Knox."

"Hello."

She stood and reached to pat what appeared to be a black, brown, and white mixed-breed dog lying on the floor.

The sight of her wedding ring brought an abrupt end to Knox's bewilderment. "Can I help you?"

"My dog…n-needs help," she stuttered.

Without a word, Knox lifted the animal to the examination table. Dominique was playing games. She didn't like dogs. She didn't like animals, period.

She stood across from him as though this animal were actually important to her. He could hear Dominique's quick pants for air.

Knox avoided eye contact with her. "What's the problem?"

"I-I found him. Near a school. Wandering. So I picked him up. He seems fine, but…I'd like you to check him out."

Knox steadied himself despite the familiar scent of Dominique's perfume. He performed a routine visual examination. Listened to the dog's heartbeat. Inspected his eyes, teeth, and underbelly. Spot-checked his skin. "He's been on the streets for a while. And he has fleas."

Dominique groaned in disapproval.

"Otherwise, he seems pretty healthy. You can bring him back Monday for blood workup."

"Umm…how old is he?"

"I'd say nine or ten," Knox guessed. "He's got another three or four years to go, possibly."

Dominique nodded. "Umm…What breed is it?"

Clearly, she was stalling.

Knox informed her, "Somewhere between a Cocker Spaniel and a Beagle. They call them Coagles. You can research them online."

"Thank you."

"You're welcome, Mrs. Collins. Shelly will finish your paperwork at the front desk." Still holding the dog, he opened the door for Dominique.

"Wait. Knox." She bit her lower lip. "I-I *had* to see you."

"Why?"

"I can't explain it," she admitted as her eyes moistened. "We were friends, you know? I miss talking to you. I'm so dramatic and you're so…calm. You always made me feel as though everything would work out. And it always did. I appreciate that about you now."

"But you *didn't* appreciate it when you walked out

of the chapel two years ago."

Dominique lowered her head. A tear fell to the floor. "Hindsight is twenty-twenty."

"Here's your dog." Knox held the animal away from his body for Dominique to take custody and leave.

"I don't want it." She sniffed. "I'll pay the bill for his checkup today. Just promise me you'll give him to someone who'll do a better job of caring for him than me. If he's hooked up with the right owners, least one of us will be happy for the rest of our days."

"Are you serious?"

"Yes."

Dominique was right. Hindsight *is* twenty-twenty. Knox could see with great clarity that she was perhaps the biggest drama-queen he'd ever encountered.

Knox cradled the dog against his waist. "Have a good day, Mrs. Collins."

Dominique ran out of the office, whimpering slightly. Knox could only shake his head.

He sat the animal back on the table. "Dude. You have no idea what I saved you from just now. That chick would have driven you crazy."

The dog's ears perked up.

Knox laughed at the four-legged friend. "Yep. You owe me. Big time."

He carried the dog to the recovery room and sat him in a cage. Knox called the nearest animal shelter. After the usual pleasantries, Knox informed the shelter volunteer that a dog had been abandoned at his office. He described the animal in great detail.

"Does she have a white tip on her tail?" the woman asked.

"Yes, she does."

"That's weird. Someone just rescued her from the shelter two hours ago."

"Wow." Knox had known that the I-found-a-stray-dog was false. But the lengths Dominique had gone through to see him again...sad. "I'll bring him by in a half-hour or so."

"Thank you, Dr. Stoneworth. Always a pleasure."

Knox found a spare kennel and loaded up the dog on his way out of the office. He said good-bye to Shelly as he left. "Don't work too late."

"I won't. Hey – are you planning to put that lady's dog down or something?"

"No. Why?"

"She was crying like she'd just lost her best friend."

She did. "She'll be fine. Have a good weekend."

"Will do."

On his ride over to the shelter, he could be nothing but grateful. If Dominique was willing to use a dog as her pawn, what would she have done with children?

He racked his brain trying to remember if there were signs that Dominique was selfish that he overlooked. She pouted every now and then when Knox refused to eat at her favorite restaurant or purchase certain big-ticket items on impulse. Knox wasn't the type to walk into an entertainment center and buy a 50-inch television without first researching the pros and cons of several brands online. Dominique, however, would see a woman at church with the latest eight-hundred-dollar purse and rush to the nearest Neiman's or Macy's after the benediction to buy it.

At the time, he simply thought that was a "woman" thing.

Maybe I just don't know how to pick a good woman. Dominique had used him for stability. Jada might have, too.

Knox parked and took the dog inside. The staff was happy to have him back, and by the way his tail wagged, Knox knew the dog was happy, too.

He wished his fellow animal-lovers well and walked back to his car.

His phone rang and "Job" appeared on the screen. He answered, "Yes?"

"Dr. Stoneworth, it's Shelly. I'm sorry to call you after hours, but someone called the backline and left an urgent message. A...Jada J—"

"Did she leave a number?"

"Yes."

Thank You, God!

Knox stored the number in his short-term memory and called Jada right away.

Her sweet voice put an end to the jitteriness he'd been feeling for the past seventy-two hours. "Knox. Thanks for returning my call."

"Where have you been? I've been trying to reach you since Tuesday afternoon."

"It's a long story. I'm at the library on Folkner Street. Can you meet me here?"

"On my way."

Chapter 12

Being surrounded by mountains of books gave Knox a flashback. Years of serious studying had him camped out at libraries many-a-night. The rows of books seemed to welcome him as he searched through them for Jada.

He found her in a section of the library marked "Computer Zone" by a bright, overhanging sign.

The seat next to her was empty. He pulled the chair back.

Jada, perhaps surprised, looked up at him with a questioning glance. Her brown eyes softened with recognition as she stood.

Unable to contain his relief at seeing her again, Knox pulled her into an embrace. Her arms pressed tightly at his sides. She must have been feeling the same.

"I've been calling you—"

"Shhhh." Jada playfully reminded him that they were in a library.

"Right."

They sat and leaned in toward one another.

"I've been trying to reach you for three days," he half-fussed in a whisper. He wanted to touch her skin, kiss her lips, soak in her beautiful presence.

"I'm sorry. Patrick killed my phone. I had to leave their house. Today was my first opportunity to get to a library so I could follow up on the resumes I sent as well as find your office number. I was praying I hadn't missed you when I placed the call after five."

"Wait. Back up. Patrick destroyed your phone?"

"Yeah. He put my sister in a choke-hold. I recorded the incident on my phone. He jerked the phone from my pocket, slammed it to the floor, and stomped it."

Knox's fists clinched on top of his knees.

Jada put her soft hands over his hands. "Don't get upset. This is between my sister and her husband. Until she makes up her mind about what she will and won't allow in her life, this is her problem. I can't take a big, black magic marker and draw the boundaries for her life."

As much as Know wanted to intervene, he knew there was truth in Jada's reasoning.

"Where have you stayed this week?"

"At a shelter."

Knox's stomach turned. "A *shelter*?"

"Yeah." Jada tried a weak smile. "It's pretty nice, actually. Women and children on one side of the building, men in a totally different part. Decent security, friendly workers. We each have our own section. Kinda. They have these partitions between spaces. Maybe four feet?" She raised a hand to show how high they were. "When you lay down on your cot, it's almost like you're in your own bedroom. A little privacy."

Knox could only stare back at her. The thought of Jada living in a homeless shelter was literally making him sick.

"Why are you looking like I just said your Labrador

Retriever died?" Jada chuckled.

He blinked and stuttered, "I—I can't believe you've been living in a *homeless* shelter."

"Umm...yeah. That's where people who don't have a place to go *go*," she reasoned. "It's not the worst place in the world, ya know? My mom was single with two kids. We spent a night or two in a shelter back in the day, before she got on disability."

"Wow."

"Knox. Please. With the economy the way it is and all these natural disasters...anybody could end up without a roof over their head at any moment."

He kept staring. A homeless shelter?

"Except people like you, Knox, who have enough siblings to form a basketball team and parents with a guest house." Jada rolled her eyes in jest. She turned her attention to the computer screen.

"I guess you're right."

Of course she was right. Between his siblings, uncles, and cousins, Knox could never imagine a day when he would have to sleep on a cot with only a 4-foot wall separating him from a total stranger. *Thank You, Lord.*

She was also right about the fact that it didn't take much for a person to find themselves without a place to stay. *Thank You, Lord, again.*

Jada gasped. "Oh great. I missed an interview opportunity. They wanted me to come in yesterday but I'm just seeing this email today." She smacked her forehead. Then she sighed. "Wouldn't have mattered anyway until I can take this band-aid off my head."

"It's been five days. Let me see." Gently, he tugged at the corner of the adhesive strip.

"Ouch!" Jada slapped his wrist.

"Be still."

"Just yank it off."

"Who's the doctor here?" Knox asked, laughing at Jada and realizing that the two of them probably sounded like an old married couple—comfortable enough to express themselves without fearing judgment or retaliation.

When he had removed enough of the bandage to determine that her smooth skin was strong enough to stand a 'yank', he quickly pulled off the remaining inch of the bandage. He tossed it in the trash can beneath the computer desk.

Knox noted the scab and the lack of swelling. "Yeah, those stitches can be removed now."

"Only one problem now. No cash-a-roni for the procedure." Jada exhaled. "And *now* I have to get a new band-aid."

Knox shrugged. "Technically and legally, you *can* remove sutures yourself."

"Really?"

"Yep. Helps to have the right tools," Knox admitted.

"Sound complicated."

"No. It's not that serious. I've got the tools at my clinic."

"*Dog* tools?" Jada retorted.

"They are not *dog* tools. They're just tools. I use them on myself all the time."

Jada smacked. "For what?"

"Anything. Ingrown toenail, splinter. Truth be told, many animals are cleaner than human beings. You'll be perfectly fine removing your stitches with our sterilized tools."

"Are you serious?"

"Yes. And you need to take the sutures out before they bond with your skin tissue."

She puffed up her cheeks then blew the air out. "Will it hurt?"

"May not be comfortable, but I wouldn't classify the experience as painful."

"You've done this before?" she quizzed.

"Yes."

"On *humans*?"

"I have three brothers. We've all done it plenty of times. I even sawed off my youngest brother's cast when I was sixteen."

"I don't think that's legal," Jada said.

"I wouldn't advise it," Knox agreed.

"Fine. Let's do this."

After two unsuccessful tries at removing the first stitch, Jada gave up. She dropped the tweezers and scissors on the metal tray and sat back in the chair, away from the magnified mirror. She and Knox were alone in a quiet but spacious examination room. "I can't do this. It's gross. And it's too complicated."

"It's only complicated because you're having to shut one eye. A focus problem since you can't see correctly without both eyes," Knox assured her. "Does it hurt?"

"No, but I don't like the tugging sensation. And knowing that I'm the one causing the sensation with my own two hands, which makes it even grosser." Jada pouted.

Knox sighed. "Proposition. I will remove the sutures. But you have to release me from all liability first."

"Consider yourself released."

She watched as Knox produced his phone from a front pocket in his black slacks. He pointed the camera at her. "Repeat after me."

Jada snickered. "What?"

"I, Jada Jones…"

Jada doubled over in laughter. She tried to block the camera with her hand but Knox, who was also laughing, moved out of her reach.

"Come on. For real. I, Jada Jones…"

Jada caught her breath but wasn't able to stop the smiles. "I, Jada…wait, cut."

"How you gon' cut on your own last name?" Knox asked.

This was the first time she'd heard Knox go southern. She liked it. "Okay. Okay. I'll try again. I, Jada Jones…"

"Do solemnly swear…"

"Do solemnly BLEEP!"

Knox's camera skills declined, the phone shaking as he responded to her joke in laughter. "Do solemnly swear!"

"Do solemnly swear."

"That I will not sue Dr. Knox Stoneworth."

"That I will not sue or knock out Dr. Knox Stoneworth…"

He nodded. "Now we have the threat on video, too. Uh huh. You think you're smart."

Jada smacked. "What else do you want me to say, dude? This confession is taking too long."

"Will not sue Dr. Stoneworth should I incur any injury having my stitches removed."

"Won't sue a brotha if he messes up. But I would not strongly advise him to mess up. Amen."

"That wasn't really a prayer, but I guess it works. Amen and amen." Knox chuckled as he put the phone away. He pointed to the stainless steel table in the middle of the room. "Up."

"Wait. Do you put pigs on this?"

"No. Only very large dogs."

"Who cleans it?"

"Maintenance staff. They'll be here in another fifteen minutes or so, probably."

"So no one has cleaned it *today*?"

"We sanitize it after every procedure. If it makes you feel better, though, I'll wipe it down with disinfectant again."

She shivered just thinking about germs. "Would

114

you, please?

Jada stood against the sink with arms crossed as she waited, watching Knox clean the table for her. He reminded her of the bus boys at her first job, the International House of Pancakes. She'd been a waiter. A terrible waiter. She had no patience for 6-year-olds who couldn't decide if they wanted a smiley face made of whipped cream or of bananas on their pancake. When the parent finally made the decision and the kid whined, it was all Jada could do not to yell, "You should be grateful your parents can afford to take you out to eat, you little princess-wanna-be!"

Jada's impatience always seeped through to her service. Tips were nill. Rude comments abounded. Waitressing was definitely not the thing for her.

"Ready," Knox announced. "Hop up."

She double-checked his work by running her fingers along the surface.

"Oh, you're going to check my cleaning skills now?" Knox huffed.

Jada giggled. "You did aiiight." She hoisted herself onto the table.

He washed his hands in the sink. He donned a pair of plastic gloves and turned on the bright light overhead.

This right here—a tall, strong man standing over her smelling of a sweet-musky cologne—she wasn't prepared for. This was even worse than at the clinic because now she knew Knox. She knew that his pleasing exterior was only the gravy on top of the goodness within him.

What if she grabbed him, right now, and pulled him into a kiss? What if he kissed her back? And what if he fell on top of her and accidentally stabbed her eye with the scissors and she went blind! But he has the video releasing him from all liability! What if— "Ouch!"

"Pain?"

She tried to relax her facial muscles again. "Tug."

"Then say *tug*, not *ouch*. You're making me nervous. I don't have this problem with dogs and cats."

"Sorry."

As Knox continued with the procedure, Jada realized she was holding her breath, her emotions, and the attraction inside. "Almost finished?" she barely mouthed.

"Almost."

She licked her lips. Seeing Knox's beautiful face in concentration suddenly made her jealous of the animals he tended to daily. He was serious about his work, totally focused on his subject.

Jada closed her eyes. Else, she wasn't going to make it out of there without embarrassing herself and, possibly, Knox.

"Done."

"Great." Jada stared up at his handsome face.

He smiled down at her.

A second of silence. Two. Three.

"I've got a mirror." Knox broke the trance.

Jada sat upright and rubbed a finger across the freshly freed skin.

Knox handed her a mirror. "Good as new."

Jada examined her reflection, noting the small holes above her eyebrow where the needle and thread had been pulled through on each side of the cut. "A little rough, eh?"

"The puncture marks will fade with time."

"If you say so." She returned the mirror. "Thank you. For everything."

"You're welcome."

"Hello!" a male voice rang.

Jada hopped off the table. "Who's that?" she whispered to Knox. Her eyes scanned the room for a weapon to defend herself.

"Maintenance guy. Paul."

"Oh."

"I'm finishing up, Paul. Be out of your way in a minute," Knox called.

"No worries. I'm starting in the restrooms."

Knox threw the scissors and tweezers into a container marked 'bio.' He grabbed his white jacket. "Ready?"

"Yeah."

"Where to?"

"The shelter," Jada said, wondering why he'd asked.

Knox's shoulders dropped. "Are you sure there's no other place I can take you? What about my parents' guest house? It's still empty."

Jada looked around the sterile room. "This place isn't so bad."

"I'm sure I could ask—"

"Knox, I'm kidding. I'm not going to stay here. The shelter is not the worst place in the world, you know? Maybe in *your* world, but not mine."

"I don't like the thought of you being there."

"It could be worse. Like at my sister's house. Let's go."

On the way back to the shelter, Knox stopped and picked up a burger and fries for them both. Grateful, Jada ate it like it might be her last good meal. "I'm healed and fed." She laughed.

Knox wasn't in a joking mood, though. The crease in his forehead had appeared when she mentioned the shelter, and it was still holding strong in place.

She directed him to the front entrance of the shelter, which was directly behind a Methodist church. "Stop here."

He put the car in park and sighed. "Jada. This is unnecessary. You know that, right?"

"Look. If I have a choice between staying at a shelter or catching a case by staying with my sister, I'll take the shelter for two hundred, Alex."

"You do have another choice. My parents—"

"Your sister wasn't too crazy about me being there, if I remember correctly. It's her parents' pool house, too."

"Is that what this is about? Rainey, who runs nothing?"

"No," Jada admitted. She'd been hoping the part about his sister would make Knox relent.

"If you're worried about her, why don't you stay at my condo? I'll stay somewhere else."

Jada huffed. "Knox. Stop it, okay? I know you're a great person with great intentions and you can't imagine the horror of staying at a homeless shelter. But you're not me and I'm not you. I can handle this. Besides…" Jada bit her bottom lip momentarily. "I don't have to stay here much longer. My mom bought me a ticket back to Memphis on the Superbus. I leave Monday."

Knox inhaled sharply. He felt as though he'd been knocked upside the head with a bag of rocks. "Wait, wait. What? Monday?"

"Yes. Monday." Jada pressed her lips together in a look that read, *This is the end of the road.*

How could she leave him right now? Or ever?

"Don't look so devastated," Jada said, tapping the end of his nose with her fingertip.

Knox wanted to grab her hand, ask her to stay. But what would he do with her? She wouldn't accept his offers for shelter. Jada wasn't into being rescued, and he couldn't force his hospitality on her.

"This is…disappointing," Knox admitted.

"It's not *disappointing*. It's *life*," she summarized. "I've been disappointed countless times. This is just another tally mark to add to all the others." She drew a short line in the air with her fingertip.

"And you're okay with it?"

"What else am I supposed to do—change the world?"

"Not the whole world. Only *your* world."

Jada gave a condescending grin. "You're so optimistic. I'm glad for you. I truly am. One day, if I ever have kids, I'll try to give them the best of everything so they can think like you. But until then, I've got to live in the real world."

She reached for the door handle.

"Wait." Knox didn't know what else he could say to stall her. He thought for a second, then he asked, "Is there anything I can do for you? Anything at all?"

Jada's eyes rolled up and to the left. "Well, you can hold a few things for me. A lady was eyeing them last night. I don't want no trouble from her." Jada unzipped her backpack and pulled out a smaller bag. "You can hold this for me until I leave."

Knox took the bag from her. It was quite heavy for its size. "What is it?"

"Some pictures. My Bible. I guess the lady at the shelter must think my Bible has some money in it. You know that old saying—if you want to hide something, put it in the Bible?" Jada laughed.

Knox didn't. He still couldn't believe he was dropping her off at a shelter of all places.

"Can you come back before Monday?"

"I'll be here tomorrow," Knox quickly replied.

"For what? I mean, tomorrow is Saturday. There's nothing—"

"I don't want you hear longer than you have to be. Breakfast. In the morning." The words came out more forcefully than he'd planned, but he couldn't help it.

Jada was frustrating him. What kind of man would he be to drop off someone he cared for at a shelter? In his mind, only those without family or loved ones lived in shelters; people who had gotten on drugs, stolen from their family members and such. Those were the kinds of people who wound up in shelters because they'd burned all their bridges.

Not people like Jada. Strong, independent, sweet, hard-working, smart.

This woman was messing up his do-good-get-good philosophy.

"Fine. Breakfast. But they don't open the doors until eight."

"What? Are they locking you in?"

Jada swung her head to face him. "It's more a safety precaution. We have to be inside by eight p.m., can't leave before eight a.m. That way, people won't come running in and out all night long. "

Knox tried to imagine the logistics behind running a homeless shelter. He imagined the chaos that might ensue with people coming to the shelter in the middle of the night, waking up those in an adjacent section. He could understand the need for these rules. "I see."

"Goodnight, Knox."

"Night."

Jada opened her door, grabbed her bag, and left him. Again.

As she walked toward the door, he saw the eyes of the men who were hanging around the entrance. They were checking her out. One of them even whistled.

Knox rolled his window down. He might have to intervene.

Jada replied to the whistler, "I ain't no dog, so don't be whistlin' at me, fool."

Surprised, Knox felt his eyebrows shoot up. He had to give it to Jada, she knew how to handle herself in this environment. Oddly, Knox found himself enamored with her ability to function in his world and this...other world he wouldn't wish on his worst enemy, let alone Jada.

As soon as Jada was inside the door, Knox shifted his gear to drive. He checked to his right, then to his left, where he saw a woman and two young girls approaching the building. The mother's hair was pulled back into a tight bun. The children were dressed in khaki pants and red collared shirts, probably some kind of school uniform.

Why are they here? Knox wondered.

"Momma, how long do we have to stay here?" the oldest girl, whose long, beaded braids clanked with each step, asked.

"Until the Lord makes a way," the mother answered. She repositioned a large backpack on her shoulders.

"How long will it take for God to make a way?" from the youngest one.

"I have no idea. But we're going to make it. Somehow."

The desperation in the woman's voice struck a nerve in Knox. These people. This woman. The

children. Jada.
This shouldn't be.

Chapter 13

With the lights dimmed to afford sleep to those who could actually lose consciousness in the building, Jada lay on her cot, thinking. She'd put up a good front for Knox, maybe even for herself, but the truth remained—this was ridiculous.

She could understand why her mother had been in homeless shelters. Running in and out of relationships, not having a profitable education, working minimum-wage jobs, and trying to raise two children as a single mom; that was enough for any woman to land herself in these circumstances.

But now that Jada had gone a step further with her education, refrained from having children, and even accepted Christ as her savior, stuff wasn't supposed to be like this.

Then again, this was the story of her life. Just as she'd told Knox, she was used to disappointment. Life wasn't a fairytale.

A soft buzzing sound emanated from a nearby section. Then it stopped.

"Shhhh!"

To which, a female voice replied softly, "The machine has a motor, you know."

"You're going to get us both kicked out of here."

Their hushed tones caused Jada to rise off her cot and get nosy. She peeked over the ledge, to the adjacent section, and immediately saw the dilemma. A woman with purple, stringy hair was tattooing a twenty-something girl's arm.

She looked up at Jada. "It's loud, right?"

The girl's eyes were already watering despite the fact there was only a small line inked onto her right forearm.

"Kinda."

"I told you," the girl told the artist.

"Hey. Will you be our lookout?" the woman asked Jada. "I'll give you five dollars."

"Up front," Jada insisted. No way was she going to do the job and then get burned on the back end.

The woman reached into her pocked and pulled out a crumpled five-dollar bill. She handed it to Jada. "Here."

"Gotcha." Jada stuffed the money into her bra. She had enough cash to make it to Monday, when she'd get on the bus, but an extra five never hurt.

Jada piled her pillow and blanket on the cot, positioning herself so that she could see over the tops of the dividers. For the next twenty minutes, she earned that five dollars and an opportunity to make a phone call on the customer's cell phone by keeping watch to make sure the shelter workers didn't sneak up on the tattooing-in-progress.

The guise of talking on the phone served well as Jada surveyed the landscape as the tattoo ensued. She called Sam and asked how she and the baby were doing.

"We're fine. Momma said you were going back to Memphis, huh?"

Her sister sounded different somehow, but Jada couldn't put her finger on exactly what was happening.

Jada answered, "Yeah. Starting fresh."

"What about Knox?"

Jada sighed. "There are more fish in the sea, I guess."

"Some fish are better than others," Sam said.

And there it was again. The way she pronounced the "f" sound.

"Joo-Joo is going to miss you. He's been looking around for you. I can tell. He cries for you, too. But he'll be fine after a while."

The difference was more pronounced that time. "Sam, there's something wrong. You sound like...something's wrong with your mouth." She'd heard about people's speech suddenly changing. "Go look in the mirror and smile. See if both sides of your face move."

"I'm not having a stroke. It's my lip."

The heat bubbled in Jada's stomach. "What's wrong with your lip, Sam?"

Silence.

"I repeat. What is wrong with your lip?"

"It's just...a little swollen. That's all."

"He hit you, didn't he? He finally hit you."

"It was a little argument. I guess I—I took things too far. I insulted his manhood and he—"

"There's no excuse for what he did, Sam. It's not your fault he has anger management issues." Jada fought to keep her voice under control and stay on watch for the tattooing at the same time.

"It won't happen again. Trust me."

"It will happen again because he's crazy," Jada countered.

"I gotta go. He's home."

The very thought of having to end the conversation because Patrick was home sickened Jada all the more. Yet, she knew that if he found Sam on the phone instead of in the kitchen or someplace out of his way, that would only make the arguing start five minutes earlier. "I'll talk to you later."

"I love you, Jada. Bye."

Saddened by the end of their conversation, Jada ended the call and slowly gave the phone back to the girl getting the tattoo.

"Drama?" she asked.

"Too much drama."

"I feel your pain, girl. Men."

"Men and needy females who have no clue what they're worth."

Immediately, Jada felt ashamed of herself for having turned on her sister, even with a stranger. But how else could she reconcile the fact that her sister was allowing her husband to abuse her?

Jada's heart jumped when another fellow homeless woman popped her head above the divider on the opposite side of a makeshift tattoo parlor. "What y'all doin'?" she whispered.

The buzz stopped as the artist answered, "Tattoos."

"Ooh. You're that tattoo lady. Can you do a

person's face?"

"You got a picture of 'em?"

"Yeah. On my phone."

Jada kept guard as the artist negotiated another deal. The second customer negotiated a fee of fifteen dollars, a pack of cigarettes, and a bracelet bearing a silver cross in exchange for a picture of her deceased mother with the words "Forever Loved" underneath.

Jada was all set to earn another five dollars. What if she did this professionally? She could be, like, a lookout girl for the mob. Or maybe she could be a private investigator. But then one day one of her clients would accidentally leak her cell number. And then instead of being the hunter, Jada would quickly become the hunted. She knew how to fight, but what if he caught up to her in an alley? And had a stunt gun? And she fell in a puddle of water and got electrocuted?

No. I can't be a private investigator. She'd have to earn this quick five dollars and be done with it.

The tattooist finished up the first customer. She gave the girl directions on how to care for the tattoo until it healed. Then she submerged her utensils in alcohol, wiped them clean with paper towels, and moved to the next section for the second tattoo.

Jada moved to the girl's section so she could be close enough to warn, should the workers come by.

Peeking over the ledge every now and then, Jada noted how the artist started by sketching the mother's face on her customer's arm. It was amazing at how well the artist had captured the picture of the mother. The wrinkles in her forehead, the dimple in her chin, even the twinkle in her eyes.

Then the tattooing started. All was going well…until Jada spotted a wiry woman who'd gotten up a few minutes earlier pointing toward her.

"Here they come," Jada warned in a low but panicked tone. She ducked and sat down next to the young girl with the first tattoo.

The girl put her freshly tatted-up arm under a pillow.

Jada heard the clinking of the tattoo artist quickly stashing her supplies.

The footsteps of a small caravan drew closer.

"Right here! She doin' tattoos and er'thang!" the snitch pointed at the artist. Then she pointed toward the section where Jada and the girl sat. "She already did that one's arm. And she payin' the other one five dollars to watch out!"

A frown covered the olive-skinned worker's face. "You know the rules. No illegal activity of any kind. All of you. Leave. Now."

"All of who?" the second customer asked. "I haven't done anything wrong."

"Raise up her sleeve and look at her shoulder. You'll see," the snitch thoroughly informed.

The tattoo artist rose to her feet. "Whatever."

"Wait. We gotta finish."

"Come with me, then." Both women gathered their belongings.

The worker looked at Jada and the girl. "You two as

well. We have a standard to keep here."

Disgusted but unwilling to argue, Jada followed suit.

As she and her three extra-homeless companions filed past the worker, Jada heard the snitch whisper to the artist, "Shoulda hired me instead."

The first customer eyed the snitch. "You'd better hope I don't see you on the streets."

"Let's go." The worker hurried them along. She opened the front door and told them they had to leave the premises. They had to be at least as far away as the sidewalk in front of the building.

Crowded together, the tattoo artist quickly became the leader of the exiles as she stated, "The way I see it, we can either go under the bridge or go in together on a motel room."

"How much is the room?" Jada asked.

"Forty, plus tax."

Jada wondered which would be better—being holed up with three strangers in a small, nasty motel room with lights and water, or camping under the bridge on the hard concrete without so much as a toilet. Plus there would be men. And men always posed a danger to women in their predicament.

"I vote for the motel," Jada said.

"Bridge," tattoo customer number one said. "Catch you all another time." She took off walking down the street.

And then there were three.

The woman with the unfinished tattoo spoke up.

"We gotta finish my momma's picture. So I say the motel. You'll have light there."

"Everybody got fifteen to put on it?" the artist asked.

"Yeah," Jada and the other woman agreed.

"Let's go get a room, then."

The three women trudged about a quarter mile to a nearby motel. Along the way, Jada learned that the tattoo artist's name was Elizabeth and the customer's name was Mya. When they got to the motel room, it was even nastier and smellier than Jada had imagined it would be. Stained carpet, a hole punched into one of the walls, and two missing tiles in the dark bathroom.

Yet, there was a sink, a shower, and a toilet.

Mya shared her bag of powdered donuts with Elizabeth and Jada. They both thanked her and devoured the midnight snack. Elizabeth and Mya took over the small, brown table, while Jada lay on top of the bedspread and looked on in awe as Elizabeth continued the artwork on Mya's shoulder.

As she tattooed, Elizabeth and Mya talked the same way Jada recalled women talk at a beauty salon. Elizabeth used to own a tattoo shop, but her boyfriend got mad at her and torched the place. With no income and the insurance company half-blaming her, she lost everything except the set of supplies she'd ordered the week before the fire. She had no family to lean on.

Jada told them about how she'd moved to Texas for a new job, only to lose it because she refused to comply with questionable directives. She told them about her sister, her brother-in-law, and her bus ticket back to Memphis to start life over again.

Mya had been on the streets since her mother started choosing men over her, back when she was a teenager. She had wanted to make amends with her mom before she died, but it was too late now.

"That's why I want to get this tattoo. To remind me of her. She's been dead for three years, but I'll never forget her. She wasn't perfect, but she was still my momma, you know what I'm sayin'?"

Jada and Elizabeth agreed as Mya's voice began to crack.

"Do you ever…pray?" Jada asked Mya.

"Pray for what?"

"Pray for comfort. Healing. So you won't have to carry the guilt and regret around with you for the rest of your life."

"Man, I can't even remember the last time I prayed." Elizabeth chuckled, her eyes fixed on her immaculate design. "All I know is it didn't work."

"How do you know it didn't work?" Jada asked.

"'Cause I'm still alive."

"You prayed to die?" Mya said, twirling her head to face Elizabeth.

"Stay still!"

"Sorry," Mya apologized. "I just never heard of anybody praying to die."

Jada hadn't either. "Why'd you pray to die?"

"Nothin' left to live for. Ready for this life to end so I can be with Jesus and God and the angels."

"And my momma," Mya added.

Elizabeth laughed slightly. "Yep. And your momma."

Jada wondered out loud, "Maybe God didn't agree with that prayer because He has better plans for you. You ever thought about opening up another shop? Or maybe you could get a booth at someone else's shop and save up until you get enough for your own."

"Yeah. I mean, you're talented enough to have a shop anywhere," Mya added. "I've heard about you. Everybody knows how good you are. You could open up a tattoo booth at the mall and, I swear, people would come from everywhere."

Elizabeth shirked. "Easier said than done."

"Didn't say it would be easy. But it *can* be done," Jada prodded.

"Look at you," Elizabeth teased, "sounding like Mary Poppins' daughter."

Jada had to admit to herself that she did sound quite optimistic…like Knox. She smiled. "Must be this guy I met. He's rubbing off on me."

"Wait? What! Rubbing—"

"No, not like *that.*" Jada giggled. "I mean…his personality. His way of thinking. He's from this really good family. A mom *and* a dad. And brothers and a sisters that all grew up in the same house. In fact, they have a guesthouse, which is straight up Fresh Prince of Bellaire stuff to me."

Mya smacked. "Shoot, if my man came from a rich family, there's no way I'd be sleeping in this cheap motel tonight. He'd have to pry me out of his life and out of his bed."

"He's not like that." Jada plopped her chin down on her crossed arms. She closed her eyes and envisioned Knox's handsome face as she spoke. "I mean, he grew up rich, but he's not snobby. He's just...happy and hopeful and he prays. And he's positive and caring and he wants the best for himself and everyone around him. Everything about him is good."

Jada noticed the buzzing of the tattoo machine stopped. She opened her eyes to see both Elizabeth and Mya staring back at her. Jada sat up. "What?"

Elizabeth said, "I do believe you're in love, my dear."

"Duh!" Mya added. "If he's so great, why are you here with us losers?"

"He did ask me if I wanted to stay in the guest house. But I didn't want to impose. I don't really like owing people favors, you know?"

"Girl, you crazy," Mya said. "I mean, if a good man came along, wanted to add to my life, didn't have shady motives, came from a good family, and maybe could help show me how to do things a positive way—*and* he can pray for me, too? You crazy. My momma would tell you you're crazy, too, if she could."

"I can't impose on his life," Jada defended herself. "I don't want him to feel like I'm using him. Besides, I don't have anything to offer him. I want everything to be fifty-fifty. Not like he's rescuing me."

"You have plenty to offer him," Elizabeth said in a

big-sisterly tone. "You're smart, you got street sense, you know how to encourage people—shoot, you've encouraged me tonight already, talking about getting back into business." Elizabeth wiped her eyes hard. "And it sounds to me like you know God, too, since you answered why He didn't give me what I prayed for. I've been wondering what was taking Him so long. Now I know. You got a lot to offer, Jada. I say get over yourself and go for this guy!"

"Amen!" Mya seconded.

Jada smiled at her cheerleaders as their words sank deep into her heart. Knox wasn't the only one who knew how to speak life into a person.

She sighed. "You're right. You're absolutely right."

Chapter 14

Knox lay on his bed, half-asleep, yawning, but still replaying the video of Jada releasing him from liability for removing the stitches. Thanks to technology, he could study her smile. Her cheekbones. The wild curls surrounding her face. The spunk in her eyes. Jada was a beautiful human being.

And she was leaving in two days.

What do I do, God?

After another yawn, he rolled over in bed and, by the light of his television screen, caught a glimpse of Jada's belongings. *What did she say was in the bag?* He remembered her saying there was a Bible, which was probably what had made the bag so heavy.

What else is in there?

Knox hadn't grown up around many females, but he knew better than to search through a woman's purse without permission. He also knew there was no better way to get to know a woman than to do this stealthy deed.

This wasn't a purse, per se, but it might hold the key to understanding Jada.

But, is it wrong to go in her bag?

Undoubtedly, the answer was yes. But what did he have to lose? Jada was leaving Monday. She would never know he went through the bag. Plus, if he found something awful like drug paraphernalia or a picture of her with some guy, he'd feel much better about letting her walk out of his life.

Knox wrestled with his conscious a few seconds more. Curiosity won the match as he reached for Jada's bag, slid it onto the bed, and unzipped. He turned on his phone's flashlight to get a better look inside.

There was, indeed, a purple leather Bible. A calculator. A set of markers. Two plastic packages of Kleenex. Nothing revealing.

He suddenly remembered that she'd mentioned pictures, but he didn't see any. *Where are they?*

The only plausible place was inside the Bible, so Knox took it upon himself to extract Jada's Bible from the bag. He turned off the flash light, then fanned through the Bible until something stopped the flow.

He grabbed a picture from the book of 2 Kings and examined it. There was a teenaged Jada standing next to a girl with the same facial structure and nearly the exact same height. From their long, gangsta braids and flared pants, Knox guessed the picture had been taken in the early 2000s. He turned the picture over and saw his impressions confirmed by the words, "Jada and Sam. Prince One Nite Alone Tour, 2002, Kansas City."

Knox laughed, thinking of how he and his brothers had to sneak to listen to Prince back in the day because their parents said his lyrics were too sexual for teenagers. "You're already riled up enough," his father had warned. "No need in adding fuel to the fire."

Knox peered at the picture again. He remembered that Sam was Jada's sister. They couldn't have been more than 15 or 16 years old in that photo. He wondered if they had snuck and gone to the Prince concert.

He also wondered how such an equally beautiful young woman had wound up in this violent relationship with her husband. Jada hadn't said anything about Sam earlier in the day. He wondered if she and her sister were talking. Had this last incident caused an irreparable rift between them? He hoped not. Prayed not. He couldn't imagine being cut off from one of his siblings for any reason.

Knox smiled, knowing that picture must have been even more near and dear to Jada now that Prince was gone.

He put the photo back in its place, then continued searching for more pieces of Jada's past. He found another clue in the book of Psalms. Jada, Sam, and their mother, as evidenced by the oversized Mother's Day card the older woman held in her arms.

Jada's mother looked incredibly young standing between her daughters. More like an older sister than a mother. He wondered how old the woman had been when she took on the daunting task of motherhood alone. Must have been extremely difficult, to say the least.

Knox whispered a prayer for Jada's mother, asking God to show Himself strong in her life and help her to enjoy her current season of life because she certainly deserved to.

A third and final picture surfaced in the book of John. Jada, Sam, and a baby swaddled in the newborn standard-issue pink, blue, and white striped blanked with knit cap. Jada was leaning over her sister in the hospital bed. The pride shined in their smiles and the love between them was evident in Jada's protective lean over both Sam and the baby.

The backside of the picture read: *Joo-Joo's birthday!*

While tucking the picture back in place, Knox noticed the highlights, circling, and writing in the margins of most of the New Testament chapters. For someone who hadn't been in the faith long, Jada must have spent hours poring over the scriptures, highlighting what hit her and jotting down thoughts and questions in the margins.

He noted her thoughts about one of his favorite passages of scripture, John chapter fourteen. Near the sixteenth verse, she had written: *Who is the helper? Where is he? I need him in my life NOW! Please send him, God.*

Knox read the verse aloud to see how Jada might have misunderstood. "And I will pray the Father, and He will give you another Helper, that He may abide with you forever—the Spirit of truth."

Re-reading this scripture with fresh eyes helped Knox understand why Jada was confused. He'd read this passage dozens of times in his life, but without a "churchy" background, a person could think that there was another physical person coming.

He lay back on his pillows with Jada's opened Bible on his chest and prayed a second prayer. He asked that even if he and Jada never saw each other again after Monday, the Holy Spirit would reveal Himself to Jada as her constant companion.

"In Jesus' name. Amen."

He must have fallen asleep after that prayer because Knox woke with Jada's Bible still in place near his heart. He quickly took in the time from the clock on his nightstand—*7:21*.

Quickly, Knox showered, dressed, and headed out the front door to his car. He viewed his text message inbox before putting the car in reverse. There were two notes. The first was a daily devotional which Knox chose to ignore at the moment. The second was from an unknown number.

This is Jada. I'm at a motel right down the street from the shelter. Call this number when you get here. Thanx!

Knox couldn't imagine why Jada was at a motel instead of the shelter. He imagined the motel was a better place. But why was she there and not where he'd left her? Who was she with? Did something happen at the shelter?

Worry caused him to drive just a little faster than normal which, according to his brother Jarvis, was probably in line with the average driver. "Man, you be drivin' like you workin' for Miss Daisy."

Thoughts of Jarvis and his wanna-be-streetwise ideas came to Knox. He thought he'd better tell someone where he was. What if Jada was playing him?

What if she was taking him to some secluded place so someone could jump him and jack his car?

Jada's not like that. He knew better about Jada. But he didn't know about whoever she might have been with at the motel. And Knox could almost hear his mother saying, "You always let somebody know where you are."

Knox called his brother. "Yo, Jarvis."

"Yeah."

"Just wanted to let you know I'm picking up a friend of mine from a motel, not too far from the M-streets. Taking her to breakfast."

"Dude, what kinda friends you got stayin' in motels?"

"A girl named Jada."

"The one who stayed in the guesthouse?"

Knox asked, "Who told you about that?"

"Who else?"

Knox already knew the answer. Rainey had always been a tattle-tale. "Yeah. She's the one."

"Well, I don't know what you've got going on with her, but you need to finish up by ten. Did you forget? We're getting fitted for our tuxedos for Braxton's wedding this morning."

Shoot! "Snap. I *did* forget. Thanks, man, for reminding me."

"This Jada chick must have your mind in a daze because you never forget stuff."

"Yeah. I guess you're right."

Chapter 15

Knox found the shelter first, then traveled about a half mile west until he ran into a motel. A seedy motel. A disgusting motel. Like the kind in one of Steven King's novels.

Quickly, he called Jada. "I'm here."

"Okay. I'm coming out. But...um...I have a few friends with me. They'd like a ride to the restaurant. If that's okay."

Friends? How did she make friends so quickly?

"Sure," Knox replied despite his misgivings.

He checked his back seat to make sure there was nothing valuable within view. In the few minutes it took for Jada to appear, Knox imagined Jada's newfound friends as gruff-looking, desperate, and smelly people with bad dental work. Perhaps even demented.

But the two women who entered his vehicle with Jada were nothing like what he'd imagined. They looked like normal people. Jeans and t-shirts. Tennis shoes. Hair in order. And when they got into the car, no one smelled badly. In fact, the women's soapy scents might have been doing his car some good.

"Thanks, Knox. This is Mya and Elizabeth," Jada said, pointing to each woman respectively. She buckled her seatbelt.

Knox resisted the urge to hug Jada. He needed to let go of her in two days.

He turned to his impromptu guests. "Morning,

ladies."

"Morning," from both of them.

Knox had planned to treat Jada to breakfast at his favorite bistro, but he guessed the menu prices would be too expensive for Mya and Elizabeth. Plus it was pretty far out of the way. Not that he was too cheap to pay for them or bring them back to the motel, but selfishly, he really wanted to spend whatever time he had left with Jada in private. They might feel obligated to sit with them if he paid their tickets.

"How's Mickey D's?" he asked.

"Perfect for my budget," Elizabeth agreed readily.

"Same here," Mya seconded.

Pleased that he had anticipated their concerns, Knox didn't have to go far to find the nearest McDonalds. He parked and opened the doors for the ladies.

"Oooh! Such a gentleman," Mya remarked. "I can't remember the last time a man held the door open for me."

"I don't think it's *ever* happened to me." Elizabeth laughed.

Jada smiled at him, making the entire morning worthwhile. Being in her presence sent adrenaline pumping through his veins.

Inside, Elizabeth and Mya ordered and paid for their own food and sat together despite Knox's offer to cover everyone's tab and Jada's offer to make it a breakfast for four.

"We'll leave you two lovebirds alone." Elizabeth winked at them.

Knox could only hope Jada would see the truth in their words and cancel that one-way ticket to Memphis pronto.

Once he and Jada were settled and had begun eating, Knox had to ask, "How did you all end up at a motel?"

Jada rolled her eyes. "Long story short, Elizabeth was giving Mya a tattoo. I was the look-out. One of the haters in the shelter snitched on us and we got kicked out for breaking the rules."

"Wait, wait, wait." Knox chewed quickly and swallowed his scrambled eggs. "First off, how is a homeless person doing tattoos?"

Jada shrugged. "The same way anyone does tattoos. People want a tattoo. They pay her, she does it."

"Yeah, but her tools. How does she sanitize them? And who in their right mind would let somebody tattoo them outside of a licensed facility?" Knox ran down the list of objections.

Jada slapped her forehead. Then she shook her head and gave him the 'you-are-so-pitiful' stare. "Knox. You're overthinking this. It's a tattoo, not surgery."

Knox fussed, "You think the germs are going to say, 'Oh, let's not infect this time. They're homeless.' I mean, doesn't anyone care about their health?"

"It's hard to care about your health when you've lost all hope, okay? When all you have is today, and tomorrow is a million miles away, you don't think about stuff like germs and an infection that *might* happen three days from now."

"*You* do think about germs," Knox recalled. "You didn't even want to use the same tools I use on dogs."

"*I* think about germs, but not everybody does."

Knox shook his head. "I'm sorry, but it's just plain crazy to let somebody break your skin with an instrument that hasn't been properly cleaned."

Jada sat up straight, agitation etched in her face. "It's a free world. People have a right to do whatever they want to do. Just because *you* wouldn't do it doesn't make it wrong for everybody else. You don't have to judge everything and everybody, you know? You're not God!"

"It doesn't take God to figure out that some things make no sense. That's why they kicked you all out. You can't break laws because you feel like it."

Jada stuffed a piece of bacon into her mouth. "I'm sure we didn't actually break any real laws. Just the laws in that building."

"True, but—"

"It's not like we were killing anybody." Jada sighed. "You are so…I don't even know what the word is but you remember that show with the mom and the dad and the two boys? It was on black-and-white TV?"

"Leave it to Beaver?"

"Yeah. That's them. Perfect. Did everything by the book. Dad went to work while Mom walked around the house in dresses and pumps all day."

"We have rules for reasons," Knox stated.

Jada swallowed her food. "You tell me. What was so terrible about a tattoo between two consenting adults? It's not like we were killing anybody."

"Yes. You were," Knox disagreed.

Her eyebrows shot up. "Really? Explain how."

It might be a longshot, but Knox wanted her to understand, so he tried. "That center is probably funded by tax-payer dollars. If people like you and your crew—" he motioned toward Elizabeth and Mya's table— "roll up in there breaking the law and the program's managers *don't* kick you out, they run the risk of losing their funding. And if they lose their funding, people lose a place to stay. So, yes, you *are* killing people's opportunity to have shelter."

Jada laughed. "Oh my gosh. You sound like me when I go chasing these crazy thoughts in my head down some horrible rabbit hole."

Knox's ears picked up on something he'd suspected all along. "Is that what goes on in your mind? A constant stream of negative thoughts?"

She frowned in thought. "I wouldn't call it negative. It's reality."

"And your reality is negative?"

"It's not negative. It's just life."

Knox tried again, hoping to choose the right words. "Has anyone ever told you that you have what you believe for?"

"Yeah, I heard about that. But bad things happen to good people, too, so it can't be true."

"I believe it is," he said.

"Doesn't surprise me," Jada snapped back. "I don't believe in all positive thinking stuff. Sounds like something Oprah would say."

"The word of God said it long before Oprah and all her people started saying it, without giving God credit," Knox corrected her.

Jada chewed on the last corner of her sausage. "Look. I'm from the hood. We don't—"

"Please. Give it a rest," he stopped her. If he heard those words one more time, he was going to lose his breakfast.

"It's who I *am*." She raised her voice and beat her chest with a closed fist. "I'm from the poorest part of Memphis, raised by a single mom, got most of my education from the school of hard knocks. My momma struggled raising us, her mother struggled raising her. But we survived, baby."

Knox felt his emotions boiling to the surface. "You wear poverty and growing up in bad neighborhoods and being raised without a father like it's a badge of honor. Well, it's not. I think it's *sad* that your parents didn't bring you into a loving family and make sure they could take care of your financial needs before they brought you into the world. It's nothing to be proud of."

Jada's nostrils flared. "Are you saying I should be ashamed?"

"No! I'm saying you need to celebrate how far you've come and try to make things better for the next generation. That's what my parents did, and their parents, and their parents. It's time to move *forward* now, not backward. But you can't do that so long as your mind is filled with negativity and you keep applying "hood thinking" to everything. It's time for something new. Time to break that generational pattern. You can't pour new wine into old wineskins."

Somehow, Knox had hoped Jada would ask him more about the wineskins. Then he could show her the scriptures. Perhaps this would be a lovely moment of revelation for Jada. An epiphany that would draw them closer.

But instead of the glow of a eureka moment covering Jada's face, her eyes narrowed to slits. She clutched her cup of orange juice. "You'd better be glad I'm saved. Otherwise, I'd throw this juice all over you."

Didn't see that coming. "Whoa. Wait. Why are you mad?"

"Dude. You can't be that dense. You just sat up here and talked about my momma like a dog. And you think I'm going to sit here and take it?"

"I'm not talking about your momma. But you said it yourself—she learned it from her mother. And probably generations before her, too. But you can make different choices. I mean, look at you. You've already got a degree."

Jada held up the hand. "Don't try to clean it up now."

Knox sat back in the booth. "Jada, I'm only saying—"

"Just don't say anything else to me, okay? It was nice knowing you. I'll be headin' on back to my hood and my hoodish ways now." Jada snatched her purse from the booth and walked toward Elizabeth and Mya.

Knox gave chase across the restaurant lobby. "Jada. Wait. How can you get mad when you're the one who's always using the word hood?"

She swiveled on her heel, bringing them within inches of each other. "Look. You got your truth. I got mine. We don't have to agree. We're not *together*. I'm headed home in forty-eight hours. It's not that serious."

Despite her words, Knox could see the tears forming in her eyes. She quickly blinked them away.

"My bag? Is it in your car?"

"I'm sorry. I was in a rush this morning. I left it at my house."

She smiled. "Nice try. Take it to my sister's house when you get a chance. She'll mail it to me."

Knox's lungs nearly collapsed. "Jada—"

"Goodbye. Beaver."

"For what it's worth, I'm sorry. I didn't mean to offend you."

Jada turned her back and told Elizabeth and Mya it was time to leave.

Both Elizabeth and Mya looked up at Knox, who felt his mouth gaping open.

"Is everything okay?" Mya asked.

"Yeah. Let's bounce," Jada repeated. "I'll be outside." She threw her food away, walked out of the building, and stood just outside the doors.

"I don't know what you said, but you really messed up," Elizabeth said.

Knox put a fist over his mouth and blew out air.

"It's like we're from two different worlds."

"Opposites attract," Mya chirped as she and Elizabeth rose with their trays.

Knox considered her words for a moment. The opposites-attract theory might have been true for some things, but when two people couldn't agree on whether life was half-evil or half-good, that might be too much opposition to overcome.

"Don't worry. I'm sure you haven't done enough damage sitting inside McDonald's for twenty minutes to kill a relationship," Elizabeth said. She patted him on the shoulder.

"We can try to talk some sense into her if you want," Mya offered.

Everything in him said he needed to stop Jada from walking out of his life, but he didn't appreciate her calling him 'Beaver.' He'd had about enough of her belittling him for having responsible, godly, loving parents and a stable upbringing.

"Thanks but no thanks. She's got a mind of her own," Knox said.

Mya smile at him. "I don't."

"Come on! Stop flirting!" Elizabeth grabbed Mya's arm and drug her to the trash to drop off their trays.

Mya waved at him.

He nodded.

They joined Jada outside and took off in the direction of the motel.

I guess that's it.

Chapter 16

Now that she was out of Knox's sight, she could let the tears flow.

"Jada! Just listen to him!" Elizabeth argued. "He's not trying to change you. He only wants what's best for you."

"What makes you think he knows what's best? He's not God," Jada said as she continued with long streams of tears and long strides down the street.

"He might not know everything, but from the looks of his car and his clothes, he knows how to make money, and that's what matters most when it comes to men," Mya declared.

Both Elizabeth and Jada gave Mya the side-eye.

"I'm serious! Which one of us wouldn't be in a better position if we had more money?"

"Money isn't everything," Elizabeth said. "But speaking of it, do we have enough for another night at the hotel, or do we need to beg for a second chance? They usually won't let you back in for a few days after a violation unless the weather's really bad."

"I've got enough for one more night. I'm headed to Memphis Monday morning."

"I've only got five dollars, but I'm gonna need that for something to eat later on," Mya said.

They slowed to pull out their cash and count to make sure they had enough for one more night.

Elizabeth produced the receipt from the previous night to make sure they had an exact amount. "We're good," she announced. "Let's go pay for another night."

With Elizabeth leading the way now, they walked for another mile through the busy Dallas streets.

"I've got another idea," Mya offered. "That guy at the desk was pretty ugly. You think he'd give us a room if I give him a little attention? Then y'all can just pay me five dollars each and keep the rest of your money."

"Save that hustle for when you really need it." Elizabeth turned her down.

Jada could only imagine how appalled Knox would have been if he'd been privy to Mya's suggestion as well as Elizabeth's reply and Jada's silence. Knox didn't understand that people did what they had to do in tough spots.

No, prostituting wasn't right. Neither were illegal tattoos. Anyone who got caught knew they had a price to pay. You take the good with the bad. That was life. Period. *Why can't he understand that?*

"I gotta use the restroom," Mya announced. "Let's go inside."

She detoured into a furniture rental shop. Mya approached one of the employees and inquired about the restroom while Elizabeth and Jada took a seat on one of the leather couches.

"This is more like it," Elizabeth sing-songed, running her hand along the brown cushion.

Jada poked out her lips. "It's nice." Not nearly as nice as the furniture in Knox's parents' guest house, though.

"Why'd you say it like that?" Elizabeth asked.

"I don't know. I mean, it's nicer than anything I've ever had. But I *have* seen better."

"Hmph. If you say so. All I know is, I was on my way to stuff like this, you know? Before I lost my business. One week, I made a thousand dollars, after expenses and everything. I was sitting on top of the world."

Jada shared, "What goes up must come down."

"That's probably true when you're attached to people who pull you down."

The large plasma-screen television in front of them turned bright red with the words *Breaking News.*

Immediately, Jada recognized the house behind the reporter. "That's my sister's house!" The banner under the reporter read: *Unidentified person or persons shot and killed at police officer's residence.*

Jada sprinted to the television set and pressed every button until she saw the volume rise.

"Neighbors say they heard two shots fired, but police aren't saying exactly who was shot or why. Of course, it's always extremely difficult when they're dealing with one of their own. We'll have a full report tonight at nine."

Sam. "Oh my gosh! I gotta get out of here. I gotta go to the police station."

"What's going on?" Elizabeth asked.

"My sister. I think her crazy husband killed her."

Jada could feel her entire body shaking. Her head was pounding. "I have to give them Sam's side of the story before Patrick tells his lies. Call 9-1-1."

Standing on an elevated block, Knox admired himself in the three-way mirror. He was the last to be measured.

He had to admit to himself that he was a good-looking man. Good morals. Good job.

Too good to be with someone who doesn't know how to appreciate me.

But his self-talk didn't line up with his heart. Despite how his ego's efforts to comfort his heart with prideful commentary. Knox knew he wasn't too good for anyone because whatever he had going for him had come from the Lord. He had to keep believing that the Lord had a good woman for him, too. Somewhere out there.

"You three have got to be the most handsome groomsmen I've seen in a long time," the attendant said as she finished marking Knox's pants with white chalk.

"Well, uhrah, what can we say?" Jarvis joked.

"Say you've got some wonderful genes," she chirped. "I should take pictures of you and put it in my online ads. I'd have customers lined up around the corner!"

"Well, as the family's agent, I can make arrangements with you," West volunteered himself.

"Man, be quiet," Knox told his brother. "Family *agent*. Please."

"Hey, I could do it. Y'all give me, say, around

about sixty percent and Stoneworth models is a done deal."

"How *you* gon' get sixty percent and you the ugliest one?" Jarvis took a stab at his brother.

The attendant, who had to be at least old enough to be their grandmother, joined in with, "I wouldn't be too sure about that."

"Oooh!" erupted amongst the brothers.

Jarvis twisted his lips to one side. "Aw, we all got jokes now?"

"I'm only kidding," the lady recanted. "There's not an unattractive one of you in the bunch. The groom was here only yesterday. Your parents must be so proud." She stepped back and looked at them. She put both hands on her hips. "But you three—no wedding rings? Your mother must be worried sick."

West pointed at Knox. "He's the oldest."

"Throwing me under the bus, huh, bro?"

The woman swiped at Knox's pants leg. "What's your hold-up?"

Knox suddenly found himself at the center of an interrogation. He shrugged. "Haven't found the right one yet."

"Hogwash!" She wagged her finger at him.

Jarvis and West fell into each other laughing. Jarvis yelled, "She said hogwash!"

Her lecture continued, "Either you're looking in the wrong place or you're missing someone who's right under your nose." Her face softened. Suddenly hugged Knox's legs. "And that someone is me."

"Oh, no. No ma'am." Knox gently pushed at her shoulders while his brothers' faces contorted in pure laughter.

"I'm only kidding." The lady backed away. "But you think about what I said." She winked at him and walked out of the room.

Knox caught his breath. Though she had said she was only playing, the way that woman held onto his legs, he wasn't quite sure.

It didn't help that Jarvis and West were practically dying.

"Whoooo! I can't wait to tell Braxton that his tux lady is in love with Knox," West teased.

"Well, she'll have to wait in line because somebody *else* nearly caused him to miss this fitting," West said.

He had a knack for talking too much.

"So. Who is she?" Jarvis asked. "And don't think about telling me that it's none of my business because it is."

"How so?" Knox grilled him.

"I've dated a lot of ladies. Can't have you involved with any of my exes. Breaks the brother code."

"Don't worry. She's from Memphis."

"It's a small world," Jarvis pressed. "What's her name?"

"Jada," West answered.

"Jada like Jada Pinkett? She's fine. Your girl as fine as Jada Pinkett, Knox?"

Why do I feel like I'm in junior high, being

pestered by my elementary-age brothers?

"First of all, she is not my girl. Thank you very much, West Stoneworth." Standing on the podium was coming in quite handy at the moment. "Secondly, you two need to stay out of my business. Thirdly, for the record, she is actually finer than Will Smith's wife and that's as far as I'm going to go with you people."

Knox flipped his collar, a move that sent his brothers into another fit of laughter.

Knox's father pushed past the white curtain sectioning off the room. "I thought I heard my sons in here getting rowdy."

"Dad, that's Knox," Jarvis said. He and West hugged their father.

"Knox is talking about some girl he just broke up with," West said.

Their father tucked in his chin. "Broke up with? I didn't know he had a new girlfriend in the first place."

"She wasn't my girlfriend, Dad." Knox stepped off the platform and embraced his father as well. "She was—"

"The guest house girl?"

Knox shook his head. "Rainey's got a big mouth."

"Don't I know it," their father agreed. "She pitched a fit because your girlfriend stayed there but we wouldn't let that Elvin boy stay there when he came to visit. I didn't like his shifty eyes in the picture she sent your Momma on a cell phone. Look like he knows how to pick locks and break in windows."

Knox couldn't help but wonder how his father

Michelle Stimpson

would feel about Jada—a girl with no qualms about sleeping in homeless shelters.

"Don't be too hard on him," Jarvis said. "Just because somebody's got street smarts doesn't mean they're all bad."

"Doesn't mean they're any good, either," his father reiterated. "You sayin' you like Elvin?"

"No. I didn't like him because he wore tennis shoes with his tux."

West interrupted, "That's how we do it now."

"Not when you're trying to make a good first impression with your girl's family," Jarvis said.

Knox had to ask, "What do you know about meeting a girl's family?"

"I've met plenty of girls' families! Just because I haven't gotten serious enough to let somebody sleep in the guest house doesn't mean I haven't met a grandmother or two at a barbecue."

Dad got back to business. "So, where is she? When will we get to meet her? You serious about her?"

Lying to his father would be of no use. "I was," Knox admitted. "But she's moving back to Memphis Monday."

"And you're gonna let her leave?"

"She's got a mind of her own."

"Those are the best kinds of women—smart, know how to put you in your place, but soft and gentle at the same time."

"Well, she's got her ticket. I couldn't stop her."

"Son, did you try?"

Knox sighed, thinking about the question? *Did I try?*

"No, you didn't," his father fussed.

Knox laughed. "Dad, how would you know? Anyway, this girl is…very different. She's from the hood, she's rough around the edges. I really thought she was gonna cuss me out at one point."

"Did she?" West asked.

"No. She didn't."

"Is she a believer?" his father wanted to know.

"Yeah. She's new to the faith, but I think she's really serious about starting a relationship with Jesus," he added despite himself. He suddenly realized that, more than anything, he wished he could walk alongside Jada as she got to know Him.

His father must have seen that desire in Knox's eyes. "Son, if you really like her that much, pray about it." He put a hand on Knox's shoulder. "Your mother and I have been praying that the Lord would let you find someone who's genuine. Someone who's not going to try to use you like what's-her-name did. And most of all, someone with a thirst for the things of God."

Jada fit everything on their prayer list, right down to the notes and questions Knox remembered seeing written in the margins of her Bible.

"Thanks, Dad." Knox hugged his father again.

"Yes. Thanks, Dad." Jarvis repeated with fake emotion lining his voice.

West repeated, "Thanks, Dad," and completed the

group hug.

His brothers were half-joking, but Knox was completely serious.

Jada was the answer to more than one prayer. Now all he had to do was get her to see the same.

Knox's phone vibrated in his pocket. Knox wiggled himself out of the group hug. There was no name, but he recognized the last four numbers from earlier in the day. "Hello?" he said, expecting to hear Jada's voice.

"Um...is this Knox?"

"Yes. Elizabeth?"

"Yeah. It's me."

"I'm so glad you called. Is Jada around?"

"Well, no. That's what I'm calling about."

Knox stepped away from his brothers and their father. "Is everything okay?"

"Jada's fine. But her sister isn't. Something happened at her house. It was on the news. We called the police and they took Jada to the station to get her statement."

"Which station?"

"Downtown. On Riverfront, I think."

"Is her sister okay?"

"I think she's dead," Elizabeth said.

Knox's heart dropped. "Okay. I'm going downtown. Thanks for calling."

"You're welcome. And Knox?"

"Yes?"

"No matter what Jada says, she needs you."

"I know," he agreed. "I know."

Chapter 17

Knox couldn't get out of the tuxedo fast enough.

After Knox explained what little he knew about the situation to his family, West and Jarvis offered to accompany him to the police station, but he didn't want to share Jada with them just yet. He needed to be there by himself. Just him and Jesus, so she would know that if she trusted Him first, she could also trust Knox.

He parked in the garage, took the elevator to the third floor, entered through the main entrance of the justice center, and cleared security. He stopped at the information desk, where it took nearly an act of congress to determine exactly where Jada might be.

The man behind the monitor narrowed it down to three locations within the building. "I can't help you any more than other. You might have to wait for a phone call, otherwise."

"Thank you."

With his heart racing, Knox double-timed the escalator steps to the fourth floor. The courts were to the left, just as he'd been told, and offices were to the right. He checked the lobby area—no Jada.

He asked the receptionist, who returned his question with a flirty smile. "Baby, I don't know where she is, but if you don't find her, you're welcome to come back here any time."

The second stop was no better. The man at that desk wanted to know who Knox was and what business he had with a potential witness.

"I'm just trying to find my girl, that's all."

"She ain't here."

"Thank you." Knox bit his tongue with that polite response.

Somebody in there *had* to know where she was. But given what he knew of Jada's brother-in-law, this entire investigation might be a huge cover-up. Maybe someone didn't *want* him to know how to get involved.

The third stop required Knox to present his driver's license. He gathered that the higher up he went in the building, the more secure the areas became. After giving his ID, Knox told the officer behind the glass exactly what he was there to do—find the woman who had given information about the shooting at the officer's house.

"Sir, at this point, she might be a suspect, for all we know."

"No. She came here to give information."

"That case is out of our jurisdiction. You're gonna have to wait until she calls you. *If* she can."

"But—"

"I'm only going to ask you one time. Please leave the premises."

Knox felt like punching the glass between them. *Who does he think he's talking to? All I have to do is call my dad. He'll make arrangements for me to see Jada.*

He lost the stare-down with the officer, but only because they were on police turf.

Knox waited until he was back on the third floor

again to use his phone. "Dad. Who do you know downtown at the police station?"

"Plenty of people. Why? What'd they say?"

"Nothing. Too much red tape. I can't even find out where she is or who she's talking to."

"Okay. I'll make a few phone calls, but it would probably be faster for you to call on God than to wait on my people to get back to me."

"You work on your end. I'll work on mine," Knox said.

Feeling like Superman ducking into a phone booth, Knox stepped out of the flow of traffic leaving the building into a window nook.

He whispered, "God. Please help me find her."

Rather than go back to his car as planned, Knox sensed that he should search outside instead. Jada didn't have a car, so there was no way he'd find her in the garage.

There were plenty of bus stops, benches, and steps surrounding this building. She had to be...*wait.*

He spotted the curls first. Sitting on one of the ledges of the massive steps leading to the entrance.

The clothes, her red shirt and black pants, were the same ones he'd seen her wear that morning.

Knox picked up the pace. "Jada!" he called.

Her face, tear-streaked and swollen, sent waves of emotion through him. He ran now, knowing that the moment he held her in his arms, he would do everything within his power to make everything okay.

When he finally reached her, Knox sat beside her

and pulled her into his arms. "Jada. Thank God I found you."

Jada sobbed, clutching his shirt in her fist. She said nothing. Just cried.

Instinctively, Knox rubbed her arm with his hands. "I'm so sorry about your sister, Jada. She must have been like your best friend."

Jada sniffed. Rubbed her face. "She *is* my best friend."

"But she's…deceased, right?"

"No. She's not dead. *He's* dead."

"Who's dead?"

"Patrick. My brother-in-law. Joo-Joo's father." With those sobering words, her face returned to the wet spot on Knox's shirt.

He tried to take it all in. Sam had been abused. She and Patrick must have had another fight, and it didn't end well for old boy.

Jada tried to wipe her face dry, but the tears came too quickly. "We gotta go get Joo-Joo from the other police station," she wailed.

"Did you tell them about Patricks' abuse?"

"Yes." Between sobs, she managed to tell him. "Someone from the suburbs came to interview me. B-but when I started telling them what they didn't want to h-hear, they said they would contact me later *if* they needed anything f-further from me."

Knox pulled her in even more tightly. "Jada. You don't have to be strong right now. I'm here for you."

"I have to be strong for Joo-Jooooo." She wailed.

"No, you don't. Your sister's in jail, your nephew is in police custody, and your brother-in-law is dead. It's okay to fall apart. I got you, Jada. I gotchu."

When Jada's grip around his waist tightened, Knox realized that, for the first time, she had surrendered to him.

And with the help of the Lord, he would fulfill those words completely.

"Let's go get Joo-Joo."

Jada held Knox's hand and his entire arm tightly as they walked back to the elevator and then to the car. Knox held the door open for her, made sure she was secure, and then proceeded to the city's headquarters. From there, they were directed to the county social services office, where, after three interviews, a thorough background check, and a prayer, a social worker finally gave Jada temporary custody of Joo-Joo.

Before the worker brought the baby into the room, Jada asked, "Did he see anything?"

"We don't think so. Officers said he was in his crib."

"Thank you." Jada sighed.

The bouncing baby boy's eyes lit up when he saw Jada. "Hey, Joo-Joo!"

He giggled with delight and hugged Jada.

"He's obviously very happy to see you," the social worker remarked. Relief swept over her face as well. "Can you come back next week and fill out more paperwork? His mother may be in custody for quite some time, so—"

"How long?" Jada asked.

"It's hard to say. Months. Years. We never know how long the lawyers and courts will drag things out. It would probably be best if you took custody, assuming his father's family doesn't contest. We need to get that settled first. Plus, there are other services to help with his insurance, expenses, and such since you've been thrust into this situation. Do you have a baby car seat?"

Bewilderment settled on Jada's countenance. "No."

"Just a second. I'll go get one."

The baby began to wiggle and look around. "Mama? Mama? Mama?" he chanted.

Jada embraced him, with tears streaming from her cheeks to the back of the baby's romper. "Mama's not here right now."

As though he understood the words, the baby frowned and poked out his bottom lip.

"Come on, big guy. You're gonna be all right." Knox held out his arms.

Joo-Joo checked Knox out for a moment. Looked at Jada.

She nodded. "He's okay, Joo-Joo."

Joo-Joo leaned past Jada and fell into Knox's waiting arms.

The social worker returned with the car seat. "Here ya go. It's one of the first things we make sure our parents have. There's plenty more help where this came from."

"I'll be back next week," Jada assured the woman.

"Great. Here's my card. Give me a few days to

contact the father's family. Let's touch base Tuesday?"

"Yes. Will do."

Jada took the card and placed it in her purse.

With Knox leading the way and carrying the baby, they reached his vehicle again in the much smaller parking lot.

The windy afternoon threatened rain soon.

Together, she and Knox struggled to set up the car seat. Joo-Joo, who was sitting quietly in the front seat, watched on.

"Maybe we should read the directions first," Jada finally suggested.

"I'm game," Knox agreed. Breathless from their useless efforts, he reached inside the box and found the manual sealed in a plastic envelope.

But Jada's cries soon took precedence.

Knox dropped the directions back into the box and hugged her. "It's going to be okay."

"No, it's not, Knox. I can't even put him in a baby seat. How am I going to raise a kid all by myself? A *boy* at that?"

"Look around, Jada. You're not by yourself."

"I can't ask you to—"

"Woman, please! You're not asking me. I'm volunteering. Now, look, I might not know how to hotwire a car or pawn a piece of jewelry, but I'm a Stoneworth. And if there's one thing we Stoneworths know, it's how to make a boy into a man. I've seen *that* all my life. I don't know how long you're going to have Joo-Joo or how long I'm going to have you, but..." he pulled her in tighter. "I'm here for as long as you'll both have me."

He felt Jada's warm hands on the side of his face. Felt her tug his cheeks downward as she tip-toed. He closed his eyes and let her initiate their first kiss. Slow and soft. Tender, yet tantalizing in the midst of all their troubles.

Jada's feet hit the ground again. She cleared her throat. "Thank you, Knox."

"You're very welcome."

8 months later

Dear Sam,

Hey, sis. I hope this letter finds you in good spirits, all things considered. Joo-Joo is doing fine. He's into e'rythang, as Momma would say. I've enclosed a picture. I also keep your pictures in his bedroom so he'll remember your face. Don't worry. He might be nearly a teenager when you get out, but I won't let him forget who you are.

I've contacted a different lawyer to see about getting another trial in another county. Hopefully, we'll get it because the deck was stacked against you. Patrick had brainwashed his co-workers into thinking he was an angel with a wicked wife at home. The truth <u>will</u> come out!

Knox and I are doing well. His brother got married not too long ago, and now mine and Knox's wedding is coming up in two months. I'm so excited. Can't wait to be his wife.

But I tell you what: my nephew is already an honorary Stoneworth! I swear, they all love him so much. Even when Knox gets on my nerves, I still know I <u>have</u> to marry him now because Joo-Joo is a part of the family! They got him so many birthday gifts it was ridiculous! He even got a bike despite the fact that his legs are nowhere near long enough for him to touch the pedals!

Joo-Joo and I have been staying in the guest house and paying rent (I found another job!). Knox's mom likes to make breakfast for Joo-Joo every single morning. I'm talkin' real, for real breakfasts! And Knox's dad reads the newspaper to Joo-Joo. And he sits there in his high chair like he really understands what the man is saying! I expect your son will be reading any day now. He loves his "Pa-Pa Reth," even if he can't pronounce the name correctly.

Momma is fine. She's still fussing because I didn't come home with Joo-Joo soon after the incident. But I told her things were better for him here. I don't want to sound bougie, but I really don't want to go back to Memphis. I mean, the city itself is fine, but the way of thinking we grew up with was not the best. Now that I'm out of "survival mode", I see things differently. Life isn't just about getting by, it's about thriving. Not letting people tell you what you can't do, but having faith that whatever God has for you is for you.

Did you know that the Bible says God can do more than we ask or can imagine? (Ephesians 3:20!) That's one of the scriptures I've memorized since I started going to Bible study. I go to church with Knox on Sundays, too, but I really like the Bible study on Tuesday nights best because we get to ask questions. There's so much we didn't know about God and Jesus. Like a whole new world has opened up! Knox and I have been toying around with the idea of starting a ministry to the homeless. To spread this same hope. To let people know that we have to have our minds renewed in Christ. Knox knows a lot about scripture and how to run things all legal, and I know what it's like to be hopeless. I can relate to people in this predicament first-hand. So, together, I think Knox and I can really be a blessing to a lot of people. But we're just praying about it right now so don't go telling Momma we've started an organization.

But enough about me. Are you involved with any ministries in prison? If not, please do. Everybody needs hope.

I want you to know that I love you. I know you're not the cop-killer people said you were in court. I don't know what made Patrick the way he was, but I know it wasn't your fault. I'm praying for you. Don't worry about Joo-Joo. He's in great hands with me, Knox, and God.

I love you, Sam. Knox and I are coming to see you next month. Per your wishes, I won't bring the baby since you don't want him to see you behind bars.

I will also make sure we go to Memphis so he can spend Christmas with Momma.

Love you forever,

Jada "future Mrs. Stoneworth" Jones

~

Did you miss Book 1 of the Stoneworth Series?
Check out *Stuck on You* and cherish the romance of Braxton and Tiffany!

Be sure to join my email list at
www.MichelleStimpson.com
to be notified when
my next book is released as well as keep in
touch about upcoming events!

Discussion Questions

1. Knox's ex-fiancé told him that he shouldn't let money determine what he does. Rather, he should determine what he wants to do and then find a way to make it happen. Do you agree with her philosophy? Why or why not?

2. Rainey is upset because she feels her parents have a double-standard for her vs. her older brothers. Did you grow up in a house with a double-standard? Should parents have lower/different expectations for sons than daughters? Are double-standards based on gender biblical?

3. When Rainey asked Jada questions about her background, Jada refused to answer them. Do you think she was justified in her refusal? Do you think Knox handled the situation well?

4. Despite all the signs that Patrick has abandoned his vows to love and protect his wife, Jada does not feel it's her place to tell Sam to get a divorce. What are your thoughts about Jada's silence?

5. Do you agree with Jada's idea that "people believe what they want to believe" or with Knox's philosophy that "people are deceived"?

6. Jada decided to pray for her sister instead of Patrick. What were your thoughts about her decision? Is it possible for an abusive

relationship to be healed? What should the victim do in the meantime? When is it time to go?

7. Rev. Whittaker's sermon about the "soul mate" theory changed Knox's focus about marriage. What were your thoughts about the sermon? What other "deceptive philosophies" have you uncovered with Bible study? [Note: The history can be substantiated in Plato's *The Symposium*.]

8. As Knox listened to his co-worker, Fritz Lewis, talk about how terrible things might get if their company merged, Knox was praying for the right words to plant or water a seed in Fritz's heart. Are you comfortable ministering to people outside of church? What does everyday ministry look like for you at work? The grocery store? A beauty shop appointment?

9. Jada covers her shape with bulky clothes because she wants Knox to like her for her mind, not her curvaceous body. Sam tells her that her curves are a part of who she is. Where would you side in this discussion? How do you find the balance between accepting your body and modesty?

10. Jada decides not to take her sister's advice due to Sam's relationship with Patrick. Do you take relationship advice from people who are in dysfunctional relationships? Would you value marital advice from someone who is in a third or fourth marriage? Why or why not?

11. Jada has a hard time believing that Knox is a genuinely kind person. Do you find it difficult to trust people? Why or why not? How does trusting God and putting our hope in Him free us to love others better?

12. At one point, Jada decided not to involve herself in her sister's relationship anymore. Jada says, "I can't take a big, black magic marker and draw the boundaries for her life." Is there some truth in that statement? Is it possible to lead a loved one out of a bad relationship if they don't want to go? What's the alternative—stand by and watch them suffer? How exactly do you pray for people who are emotionally or spiritually blind? Do you have scripture reference for such prayers?

13. Jada told Knox that it was hard to care about tomorrow when you're hopeless and all you have it today. Do you agree? Does it make sense, then, the people would risk infection or even more when they can't see past the moment?

14. Jada had a habit of imagining the worst-case-scenarios. How does her negative thinking habits impact her life? Do you take captive of your thoughts (2 Corinthians 10:5), or do you allow them to run wild like Jada does? Do you believe that your thoughts shape your life in some way?

15. Knox accused Jada of wearing her rough

upbringing like a badge of honor when, in his opinion, it only spoke to how irresponsible her parents had been. Do you agree with Knox at all? Were you tired of hearing Jada say that she was "from the hood", too?

About the Author

Michelle Stimpson's numerous works include the highly acclaimed *Boaz Brown*, *Divas of Damascus Road* (National Bestseller), the award-winning Mama B series, and *Falling Into Grace,* which has been optioned for a movie of the week. She has published several short stories for high school students through her educational publishing company at WeGottaRead.com.

Michelle serves in women's ministry at her home church, Oak Cliff Bible Fellowship. She regularly speaks at special events and writing workshops sponsored churches, schools, book clubs, and educational organizations.

The Stimpsons are proud parents of two young adults—one in the military, one in college—and a weird Cocker Spaniel named MiMi.

Visit Michelle online:
www.MichelleStimpson.com
www.Facebook.com/TheMichelleStimpsonPage

More Books by Michelle Stimpson

Christian Fiction
A Forgotten Love (Novella) Book One in the "A Few Good Men" Series

The Start of a Good Thing (Novella) Book Two in the "A Few Good Men" Series

A Shoulda Woulda Christmas (Novella)

Boaz Brown (Book 1 in Boaz Brown Series)

No Weapon Formed (Book 2 in the Boaz Brown Series)

Divas of Damascus Road

Falling into Grace

I Met Him in the Ladies' Room (Novella)

I Met Him in the Ladies' Room Again (Novella)

Last Temptation

Mama B: A Time to Speak (Book 1)

Mama B: A Time to Dance (Book 2)

Mama B: A Time to Love (Book 3)

Mama B: A Time to Mend (Book 4)

Mama B: A Time for War (Book 5)

Mama B: A Time to Plant (Book 6)

Someone to Watch Over Me

Stepping Down

The Good Stuff

The Blended Blessings Series (co-authored with CaSandra McLaughlin)

Trouble In My Way (Young Adult)

What About Momma's House? (Novella with April Barker)

What About Love? (Novella with April Barker)

What About Tomorrow? (Novella with April Barker)

Non-Fiction

Did I Marry the Wrong Guy? And other silent ponderings of a fairly normal Christian wife

Married for Five Minutes: Hope for Living Inside Real-Life Marriages

Uncommon Sense: 30 Truths to Radically Renew Your Mind in Christ

The 21-Day Publishing Plan

Made in United States
North Haven, CT
03 July 2022

20893787R00107